IN LIGHT OF THE NEW MOON

A.J. PRUFROCK

ISBN: 978-1-7362968-0-6

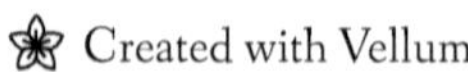 Created with Vellum

For my four

VOL. I THE LIGHT PRINCESS

EXPANDED, EMBELLISHED, AND ARBITRARILY ANNOTATED

CONTENTS

FOREWORD

The tale I am about to tell is not my own. It sprung from the creative imagination of good, old, George MacDonald.[1] He penned it (literally, there were no keyboards) during a simpler, more polite era, one hundred and four years before I was born.

MacDonald was no wordsmith. He did not write high literature but wrote fast literature in order to feed a large family. This caused much of his work to go to print hackneyed and unpolished. In spite of poor form, his books sold because his imagination was prolific.

While I did not stray too far from the original plot, I did fill in many before now untold details. MacDonald omitted, for the most part, the motivations of villains and heroes. In his day, psychology was an undeveloped field—characters *were* what characters *did*.

That said, if you are seeking tales of infidelity, serial love triangles, pet abuse, and opium addiction, I'm afraid my version of Old MacDonald's (who never sang a single e-i-e-i-o) tale is not much juicier than the original. This is not a tell-all (only

MacDonald could have done that if his eleven kids had given him time to do rewrites), it is a tell-more.

One last note—MacDonald was no poet yet wrote poetry anyway. Even in an era when sonnets sold, he had to insert his verse into his prose to get them to print. I, a desperate poet at heart, have done the same. Hopefully my rhymes do not distract from my updated, appealing-to-the-masses retelling of *The Light Princess* (1864).

Sincerely,

A.J. Prufrock

CHILDLESSNESS AND DRAGONS

THERE LIVED a king so long ago, memory of him and his kingdom are but a faint wisp in a cloud of hazy recollection. The king ruled over the land of Lagobel, which name is a proper noun that loosely translates "wrested from the claws of a dragon." King Fenton no longer believed in dragons but he had listened raptly to his grandfather spinning mesmerizing tales of the great creatures. Grandpa Kenterick knew their breeds and genealogies better than those of his own human family. He told how the Rekiki, yellow-eyed and green-scaled, preferred the meat of trolls over humans. He described the great fang and claw of the Sarkani and how, though they had no roar, they struck terror by their mere presence. Best of all, Grandpa Kenterick told of how his father's father had not killed but had outwitted a great sagacious Zenido, black as night with claws of silver. The great beast was so ashamed of his defeat that when he flew from Lagobel lake he cried and filled it two feet deeper with his tears.

Fenton's older sister memorized every detail of dragon lore, drew pictures, and charted genealogies. She did not waver in her interest even well into adulthood. When she left home, she packed her vast self-made library of winged serpents with great care while her other belongings lay strewn about. No tears were shed by her nor anyone who watched her go. Rumor had it she spat, but none of that moisture made a measurable difference in the volume of the lake.

For King Fenton, the once glorious serpents, and those who conquered them, were a faded part of his beloved but now forgotten childhood. He had practical matters to see to like counting coins, of which he had vast quantities, and progeny, of which he had none. No children had been born to the king and queen of Lagobel and they had been married many years.

At the time of our story, there was no longer any crisis in Lagobel over the infestation of dragons, but, like with so many royals, there was a problem with succession. No babies in the palace did not just mean there would be no royal grandchildren for the king and queen to spoil in their old age; it meant an empty throne. Empty thrones most always lead to chaos.

The barren royal couple lived atop one of several lovely hills surrounding the famous dragon-tear lake. Encircling the hilltops were dense trees, deep woods, thick thickets, and an abundance of wildlife. The citizens were simple and the wealth of the realm just below average compared to neighboring kingdoms. This below-par ranking kept Lagobel off the "to be conquered" list of surrounding nations and the status suited the king and queen. Lagobel monarchs lacked the fire of ambition and standing armies were thereby kept to a minimum. In other words, if no one is fighting for your stuff, you don't have to worry about defending it.

King Fenton followed the customs of his forefathers and blamed his wife for the lack of sons and daughters. Queen Ita bore the blame well, as was also custom. The queen did not trouble herself to show the king his narrow-mindedness, nor did she expect her own sorrow in the matter to enter his mind. She simply asked for his patience. Waiting did not come naturally to either of the royal couple, but Ita knew, in the matters of pregnancy and child-rearing, patience came to bear in both, like it or not. In short, the king blustered and complained and the queen kept quiet.

When at last a lovely little princess was born to the couple, neither Queen nor King showed signs of having gained much wisdom from the wait. Like the pains of childbirth, the trial of deferred hope was forgotten. Both Fenton and Ita thought they had finally gained their happily-ever-after. But child-rearing proved an inescapable taskmaster. Living *with* the longed-for princess required the virtue of long-suffering for both mother and father. Parenthood, as it does so often, tested every weakness of their marital bond. The little lovely darling precious princess nearly drove her parents, and everyone else in the palace, crazy. The couple had to cooperate constantly to avoid both public shame and private tragedy. Both eventually became unavoidable.

INVITING BAD BLOOD

A BIG BELIEVER in sacraments and sealings, King Fenton called for an eighth-day christening. He wrote the invitations himself. Determined to compose a personalized limerick for each guest on the list, he sat at his marble-topped ebony desk and twirled the long ends of his auburn mustache. A glass fountain pen lay beside three colors of ink: red, blue, and green. He had intended to use the peacock quill but the feathers kept tickling his nose and blocking his view of the parchment. The extra flair, as it so often does, was impeding artistic progress.

Fenton took off his reading spectacles, rubbed his eyes, and cracked his knuckles again and again. He had reached a point of poetic honesty learned repeatedly but never retained. After the first five limericks he was forced to admit his slow progress was not the peacock feather's fault. The guest list was long and contained impossible-to-rhyme names. "Before our next child," muttered the king, "I will pass a law against foreign sounding and multi-syllabic names. Jingleheimenschmidt—preposterous! Quattlebaum—a mockery! Schaufelberger—ridiculous!"

First names were less cumbersome but still disheartening.

He had not gotten out of the Cs alphabetically and already Aibreann, Branagh, and Caoilfhoinn had proved impossible. How can you find a rhyme for a name you can't pronounce?!

The queen had hinted the task was insurmountable, with less than a week to go and a guest list of hundreds. But the king had bragged and blustered so about his poetic abilities, there was no going back. Pride drove him on. The Earl Thomas of Adelson was first on his list. Below is the invitation sent, hand-written on the kings own stationary and by his hand—

A daughter was born to the queen
Sweet baby, royal daughter, a dream
Please come Tom and Lu
If you've nothing to do
To our grand high and holy christening

The 6th invitation was much more subdued. The king slipped unabashedly into haiku—

Come to the chapel
A sacrament of import
Dearest John and Barb

By the last twenty-five the king was exhausted. His valet (though this information is top secret) took the pen from his master's sleeping hand and wrote in his best script the same message two dozen times times—

O beloved honored guest
Royal baby to be blessed
Come to the chapel half past eight
Show this card at castle gate

The trusted servant said nothing of the matter to the king but did procure his signature which, a generation later, was worth a tidy sum.

The king's obsession with creativity had a tragic drawback. It made him unorganized. And when one is unorganized, one comes across as forgetful. And when one is forgetful, one comes across as careless, which unfortunately some interpret as uncaring. And though both words share the same root, they mean very different things. King Fenton was careless, and in his carelessness he overlooked a critically important invitation.

An invitation was not received by someone looking for a chance to be offended, and those looking for such a chance for offense almost always find it. Unfortunately, and pivotal to the pathos of our tale, the person looking for a chance to be offended was a person of power.

King Fenton's sister, Princess Vespa[1] had good grounds for being on the hunt for offense. She had been cut from her father's will. She was the oldest child but the kingdom had gone in full to her younger brother. It mattered not to her that little brother had no part in the decision.[2] It was enough that he benefitted from it. Adding insult to Vespa's injury, the cutting her out of such an auspicious document had not been delivered in proper form. She had a second beautiful reason to relish being offended and it made her wicked heart warm.

It was custom for royalty to communicate to one another in rhymed iambic pentameter[3]. However, instead of a courtly poem written in proper verse, Vespa's father had cut her out of the will with a low form of rhyme found only in the barbaric north—

Vespa, Vespa full of dread
How you wished your father dead
I'm well aware you loved none well
And hope your father rots in ____

Not only was the message crass, the verse was insulting, the meter was an affront, and the rhyme scheme off-putting.

The king, Fenton and Mary Ellen's father, had thought his poem very funny. In fact, his last sound before dying was chuckling at his own cheekiness. But under the dark humor lay unforgiveness. The legacy left by the old dead sovereign was that his offspring would pay for his bad poetry written with an angry heart. It is true that his daughter was difficult and had lost her right to the throne by her own poor choices. But the father's bitterness had caused a bitter schism between siblings. Fenton had done his best to heal it but to no avail. His big sister moved out in a huff, spat in the lake, and refused to speak to anyone at the palace.

On the day of the christening, despite having no invitation, Vespa combed her tangled salt-and-pepper hair and pulled it back into a bun so tight it straightened the deep crow's feet around her eyes. She took the time, a first in her long life, to pluck her great and mighty unibrow. It had not only grown together across her protruding forehead but had ventured low enough to become entangled in her eyelashes any time she blinked. Which was not often.

Vespa felt warm inside. She was going to see a baby and have a little fun, her first public appearance in decades. One of the last twenty-five invitations had been easy to forge so coming through the gate had posed no problem.

When King Fenton saw a lady of stature glide in, dressed head to toe in yellow, she seemed familiar. She felt familiar. The matronly figure by confidence alone made her way up to the baptismal font into an area exclusively for family. By sporting two eyebrows instead of the usual one, she threw off those pondering her true identity, including her baby brother the king.

As the priest immersed the baby princess, once, twice, three times, Vespa dipped the end of her littlest finger in the font no more than a quarter centimeter.

Instead of joining in prayer, Vespa, finger resting on the surface, breathed out in a whisper—

> *Enter not the heavenly light*
> *All heart's sorrow put to flight*
> *Weight of wisdom now eschew*
> *Weightless now thy body too*
> *Enter thou a thoughtless ease*
> *All instruction turn and tease*
> *No prudence pondered brought by tears*
> *Fulfill thy parents' unknown fears.*

Vespa then repeated the rhyme a second time in a normal tone. Family started to take note.

Finally, in a dramatic exit, Vespa spun through the crowd, screeching the rhymed octave in operatic catcall. Damage done.

Queen Ita watched her go and resented only slightly what she perceived as a grab for public attention. Rhyme and verse belong in the theatre. Why must drama intrude into the chapel? she thought to herself, shaking her head until the royal crown slipped slightly. She abhorred Vespa's noise, thought her sister-in-law's bizarre twist of a phrase doubly ignorant on such an important occasion, but then she saw the rhyme's effects.

Her baby girl floated. And giggled. [4]

[3]

HAPPINESS DESERVED

VESPA, as you might have guessed, had abandoned all semblance of faith and humility long ago, instead embracing raw power of the darkest sort. The health of her own soul was of no consequence to her, so nothing held her back from a life consumed by envy and revenge. In complete dedication she perfected her manipulative craft.

At first her curse seemed harmless. She was just a crazy old lady on a lark. 'Twas but a joke, a parlor trick soon to wear off. Had the baby caught fire, the palace guard would have pounced. Had baby Ethereal shriveled and screamed, all hope of escape would have been cut off. Had Vespa dashed the child to the floor, a dungeon, not a pleasant walk home, would have been next on her agenda. But who arrests a guest, even an uninvited one, for making a baby levitate and giggle? Isn't happiness what everyone is after? Vespa had simply given the royal couple exactly what they wanted, just in fuller measure than they ever expected. She smiled as she walked; she let her hair down allowing her crow's feet to return to their natural posi-

15

tion. She would have skipped home if her arthritic knees would have allowed for it.

The queen had prayed for a happy baby, and had hoped, if she were a girl, she would be the charming life of the party. Over-serious Ita had almost been left behind when it came to family life and marriage. She over-thought and over-felt which led her to being over-educated. Her inability to keep her nose out of the books was most unbecoming. What prince wanted a brainy wife? The death of Fenton's first wife had made him lonely, and willing to overlook his second bride's propensity to ponder. She did not wish this burden upon their daughter. She had, in unknowing silent agreement, sealed the spell cast by her not so pleasant sister-in-law.

The curse affected little Ethereal with lightheartedness of both body and soul. Everything under the sun and moon made her happy, as if euphoria was poured into her pores, forcibly. The lightness of Ethereal's spirit infused her little body as well. She giggled at feeding. She chortled at diaper changes. She laughed when staff played peek-a-boo. She laughed when she was left alone. She even snickered in her sleep.

The infant princess commanded her own set of physics. To rock her was to risk, by the least looseness of grasp, rocketing her across the room. Usually, and thankfully, the simple resistance of inside air slowed her propulsion to a simple float before she crashed into wall or ceiling. A small step ladder was kept in every room with a vaulted ceiling, for it was all too common one needed it to fetch a baby down. A satin harness was soon affixed to the princess so if her weightlessness fooled her carrier, a loop around the wrist of a nursemaid or nanny provided a mooring. She was a boat that floated upward, always in need of an anchor.

When the princess was pressed weightless in her father's arms for the first time, he turned white. Quite sure of his own weightiness, the king then turned to his faithful queen and faltered, "Are you sure she is mine?"

It was a desperate, shameful moment of weakness. A less secure wife would have wept or pouted or gone into hysterics at the mere hint of accused infidelity.

The beautiful truth was, and this is unfortunately rare among royal families, not only was Queen Ita body-and-soul faithful to her husband, but King Fenton possessed a rare faithfulness to his wife. The king had no secret girlfriends on the side. Not because he could not, for people turn a blind eye to the affairs of their male sovereigns, but because he did not want to. Like Ethereal, whose body and soul were both the same—lighter than air, the body and the soul of the king and queen also possessed integrity. For all their faults, they did not say one thing and do another. If this had not been the case, I doubt this story, for all its heartache and struggle, would have anything close to a happy ending.

Because of this simplicity, Queen Ita did not falter in any emotional turmoil. Ignoring completely the king's ludicrous question, "Are you sure she is mine?" she went to the heart of the real problem. She turned to husband and said, "I think, dear one, that we should have been more careful at our daughter's christening."

The king put both hands to his mouth and gasped. In so doing he released the little princess whom he had forgotten to secure with a tether and forgotten that he was holding in the first place. As Ethereal floated upward servants scrambled for ladders and the baby exploded in laughter. The king, used to others cleaning up after him, held on to his eureka moment.

"Vespa!" he moaned, "The octave she recited was a spell ... my darling queen, I know what happened."

"And somehow my wishes for her to be light-hearted

helped in the bewitchment," murmured Ita to no one in particular.

Her comment was drowned out in the explosive giggles of their daughter, who had been caught just as she was about to float out an open window.

[4]

DOWNSTAIRS UP

As in most palaces, the lower floor in Lagobel was populated by the servant class. The little princess brought up the spirits of those living below in the exact opposite fashion as she brought down the spirits of those living above. Footman, butler, milkmaid, and housekeeper all adored the new little charge. The poor nanny was almost out of a job for who does not want to get their hands on a happy baby?

The servants had a ball with Princess Ethereal ... literally. If you heard peals of laughter from any of the rooms you could be sure the princess was, in her weightlessness, being batted back and forth in some great game of baby badminton. Rackets of different size and shapes were being tried out when the nursemaid burst in and reestablished authority. Groom and stable boy were admonished with sharp tongue until the nanny was made to see the joy was mutual. Ethereal was hysterically happy to be in the center of the game, not minding in the least that she was the shuttlecock. A compromise was hit upon: feather dusters only were to be used as rackets.

In truth, all the servants loved the little ball of fun more than the game. But all their attentions made the nanny grow lax. She had to fight to do all but the least mentionable duties. Thankfully the contents of the princess's diaper did not float about and make her job untenable. Once an item, whether it be hair follicle, fingernail, or waste product, left her royal highness, it gained the rules of the rest of the physical universe. Each weighed exactly as should be expected when free of her. But as long as an item was in contact, whether clothing or blanket or toy, the rules of gravity were governed by her little majesty. Ethereal Rules (as they came to be known), the laxness of her nanny, and a hot summer day all came together to create what was to be called "The First Great Scare."

Nanny Moninne had replaced Nursemaid Tannoch. Tannoch, though well-seasoned and experienced, could not adjust to a child in her charge floating about. She could not stop crossing herself and muttering, "Lord have mercy" every time she picked up the gravity-free infant. Proper crossing (and Tannoch knew no other kind) caused her to loose her grip on her charge, necessitating more and more often the fetching of the step stool. Tannoch was too old to be climbing about. She was too old to change her devotional habits, and she was too old to not take the whole situation quite seriously. It was a spell after all. Dark powers were afoot.

More quickly than the queen preferred, Tannoch retired herself to a nearby monastery[1] and young Moninne was promoted from milkmaid to nursemaid. A natural promotion, if you think about it.

Nanny Moninne was of a lighter disposition than her predecessor. She crossed herself less often and was more sympathetic to the personality of her charge. She allowed the other servants their fun. One afternoon though, she took their ball from them and carried her upstairs, insisting quite rightly that the princess needed a nap. The day was sultry, so sticky hot that all clothing clung. Though she could not do the same for herself, Moninne removed every stitch of raiment from the baby. Ethereal lay *over* the bed, not *on*, mind you, in her birthday suit, but the room still felt oppressive. Determined to make her little charge comfortable, the shutters were thrown open and the sashes thrown up so what little breeze their might be could come in and cool the room. Moninne stood on the stoop admiring the view of the lake, her back to her young charge. The breeze was gentle and flowed in making everything smell fresh. It flowed in, lifting the sleeping princess who was hovering over the bed. The wind, cradling her gently, transported her out the opposite open window. Moninne, lost in thought and mulling the ease and joy of her new position, did not turn round until Ethereal had disappeared across the open blue sky.

So used to chortles and chuckles, the staff below deck had their hair stand on end when they heard the scream of terror coming from the hall lined with royal bedrooms. The queen put down her toast and honey and came bounding from the adjacent parlor. One look at Nanny Moninne's face and Ita, in contrast to her whole history of keeping her wits and quashing emotions, fainted dead away. The king, in contrast to his whole history of losing his wits following his emotions, led the charge instead. Fenton nearly knocked all the coins in his counting house over, put on his sword, and called for his swiftest steed.

This time, as in so many previous games of "Find the Baby," there was no trail of laughter to guide the search party. Ethereal, exhausted from the latest ball game, remained asleep on the wind that carried her. Weightlessness was her usual state and it did not matter to her whether she rested her head over a fluffed pillow or a puff of air. All felt like nothing. Neither care nor sorrow found an entry.

The entirety of the palace staff abandoned the palace (the

queen awoke from her faint with no one to attend to her nasty goose egg) on the great mission. Eventually stable boys, who knew the woods quite well, spied the princess nestled in the arms of a great beech tree. Arms of her nurse, arms of a beech, it made no difference to the little girl and heights were not different to her than the heights of cathedral ceilings. Many volunteered to make the climb but Moninne insisted and tucked her skirt into her stockings to show her determination. The act of bravery saved her job, for the king, much afraid of heights, interpreted her efforts as penance and graciously granted forgiveness. All agreed that none should speak of the fiasco in the future, but such agreements, among so many, are pointless.

King Fenton was handed down his daughter and he waved off the staff, insisting all go tell his wife of the good news. In doing so he gained for himself a rare moment alone with his daughter. Here, with only the beech tree listening, he began to weep. He wept for the near loss of her. He wept for what might become of her. He wept for reasons unknown. The king might have stayed all night, lost in a nameless sadness, private tears falling on his daughter's weightless body, but he thought he heard a voice overhead in the branches. Birdsong and wind in a murmur drifted down, "I may love her, I may love her; for she is a princess, and I am only a beech tree."

Not liking the reminder of how wide and wild the world was, the king sought refuge inside his palace doors. Fenton walked in and handed Ethereal to Moninne with an air of indifference, pretending not to notice the concern in the faces of his closest staff over the lateness of the hour. He immediately busied himself in concern for his wife, insisting that he himself hold the poultice to her aching head. Monnine slipped in quietly and out quickly, wisely placing Ethereal in her mother's arms.

UPSTAIRS DOWN

It took less than a day and a half to restore the good-natured games of toss and giggle in the cellar and first floor. It took a full three weeks to restore Nanny Moninne's jovial spirits. She watched the royal couple closely to see whether the tree climbing rescue had indeed restored their faith in her. She received no overt assurances of their continued favor, but the king and queen were too relieved to look backward and find fault. They were also too distracted with the ongoing anxiety of parenting an exceptional child to launch an investigation. Time marched on without a word on the matter and Moninne remained in charge of one princess rather than being sent back to the care of twelve or more cows. Climbing a dozen stools to fetch a single baby was much easier work than sitting on a single stool with one's hands on the underside of a dozen bovines (and one's feet in who knows what). She crossed herself in thankfulness, but did it left-handed. Her right arm remained steadfastly dedicated to the weightless Ethereal.

The servants were happy but the queen was crying again. The usual pleasure and distractions had no charm. The king bravely went to see his wife, though he engaged her in a cowardly fashion. He entered the parlor where she sat with a tear-stained face, needlework in her lap, staring out a bay window that faced the lake. One of her hands absently brushed up and down the velvet crimson curtain. Fearing more tears, Fenton tried to be light.

"Ethereal is neither down a well nor up a chimney, my darling. Why should you be low?"

Ita answered not.

The king stepped forward and joined his wife in the beam of sunlight and tried again, "It is a good quality to be light-hearted. Our daughter certainly is that."

"It is a bad thing to be light-headed," answered the queen, looking mournful, sighing with the soul of a prophet.

Fenton ignored her tone, placed a courageous hand on her shoulder and continued. "She will be light-footed! Imagine her dancing at parties, we shall have such a great coming of age ..."

"But she will be altogether light-minded," she said stiffening. Fenton's hand fell to his side as his courage left him.

Feeling he had done more than his duty—he had come, he had made a dutiful attempt—the king turned on his heel to return to the counting house, determined to enumerate every coin if it took him a fortnight. He was not halfway to his hideaway when his queen's voice overtook him.

"It is a horrible thing to be light-haired!!" she screamed.

Now the queen's hair was black as night and the king's had once been golden like their daughter's. But this was not the point. The queen aimed to insult using the double meaning of light-haired and light-heired. She was stabbing back, finally, long after her husband could possibly recall his degrading implication months before. He really had hurt her when he suggested, however off-handedly, that the baby might not be his.

Next, King Fenton did something truly courageous, an action that would rank in the top five acts of heroism in his life (so far). He turned and went in the direction of emotional pain, pain he may have been the cause of and his wife was now in agony over.

Upon entering the room, he saw a woman so broken and rueful of her outburst towards him that he could do nothing but take her into his arms and let her weep. So he did.

In less than a quarter hour, both were spent. Marital unity had been strengthened not weakened in the sorrow. Hankies were found.

"You clearly are not bearing up as well as I had supposed," began the king gently.

"No, darling, I'm quite depressed. Even the honey pot has lost its glow. I have no appetite," said the queen dabbing her eyes.

"What is to be done!" returned the king, growing desperate and agitated.

"You might try, darling," sniffed Ita, "and I would do it for us if I could ... an apology."

A long knowing pause ensued.

"Say sorry to my sister, you mean," the king said in a whisper.

"Yes," said the queen, quieter still.

To Ita's surprise, her husband did not argue.

He stood immediately and said, "Quite right. I will go at once."

And he did go at once. Truth be told, after a man survives his wife's tears, there is no fear of a big sister's jeers. In fact this, his first real show of courage, became a line in a hit song several years later.

> *Once a man faces his tender wife's tears*
> *What terror can top him? yo ho*
> *Nor dragon nor caldron nor loss of career*
> *Can shake down his courage, yo ho*

But I get ahead of myself.

[6]

VESPA OPENS AND CLOSES THE DOOR

FENTON KNEW his sister would be delighted to see her baby brother ride up plain-clothed, on a brood mare. He also knew all self-humbling only whetted her appetite for more. As he stepped into her hovel of a hut, he braced himself for the impending exhaustion.

Fenton had offered Vespa better quarters, but she had refused. A decade ago he had built her a house overlooking the lake complete with servants' quarters. She would not move in. He then sent her workmen to make her whatever abode she wished in a place of her choosing. She called down curses upon them. The king finished arguing and offering long ago. Older sister was not interested in what was freely offered.

Without giving Vespa a chance to offer the customary greeting due a king, and knowing full well she would not anyway, Fenton prostrated himself face down before her on the dirt floor. Vespa balked, but the cat did not. The creature sniffed his fingertips, nibbled his boot straps, then curled up in the middle of his back, purring.

From the floor, Fenton wept. The dirt cleaved to the tears and mingled with the grey in his beard.

"I beg you dear sister to forgive my oversight. Please remove the spell."

"What?!"

The king repeated himself.

"I beg you dear sister to forgive my horrendous oversight. Please remove the spell upon my daughter."

"I cannot discuss these matters with you face down in the dirt. You must have a seat."

"I cannot get up ... the cat."

The cat only seemed small but was in truth quite weighty, equal to a newborn calf.[1]

Vespa lifted the feline off of her sibling and Fenton sat up cross-legged in the dirt. He was offered a stool but refused. He came to humble himself and humble himself he would.

"One thing at a time, dear little brother," Vespa said in an almost childlike sweetness, "first, give me my limerick."

Her face was set. There was no getting round.

The king should have rued the day any of the invitations were in this format, but instead he secretly exulted because, when not pressed to hundreds in a single week, he could pull limericks out of thin air. It was a gift and his gift was now being tested under extreme duress. With much more merriment than the present situation called for, he quipped—

> *Dear Vespa, please come to the palace*
> *I will serve you sweet wine from my chalice*
> *Grand sister, in peace*
> *Come bless your dear niece*
> *We're christening our dear daughter, Alice.*

Upon hearing the name of the princess a small smug smile

passed over Vespa's thin lips and her fingertips brushed lightly over a book of runes.

Little brother frowned. It was not his best limerick.

Both sat in silence for some time.

It is a dangerous thing to sit alone in an evil place with an evil person. The king knew this without knowing it and grew restless. He broke the silence,

"Please remove the spell," he breathed, feeling the choke of tears returning.

"Silly boy, I don't know what you are talking about," said his sister. Her eyes shone with a deep emerald color. "Is there something wrong on the home front?"

The king was struck. What little hope he had jumped out the window with the cat. He rose and left the way he came, through the front door. The meeting was over.

His sister called out after him, "I have several books on child-rearing if you are interested. Girls are particularly hard. One of the reasons I chose to remain childless …"

The king had lost all dignity but he did not care. If he had known what dark magic he had escaped, it might have been a small consolation. His sister's runes found no hold on him because they found not pride by which to enter.

The king returned home crestfallen. Ita tried to comfort him to no avail. "Perhaps, when our girl is older and can tell us what is like to live without gravity, she can suggest ways we can help."

Fenton, with a mind towards his legacy, did not hear. Borrowing concern from the future, he thought of generations to come and imagined his descendants floating about like hundreds of gossamer butterflies. There would be no playing on the floor with grandbabies. They'd all be above him drooling down and laughing.

Both thought of but could not bear to speak the suggestion

of consulting the court physicians. Each was afraid of experimentation.

[7]

LITTLE MISS LAUGHS ALOT

WHILE IT IS QUITE charming to hear the laughter of a baby, there is something odd when it continues untempered into adolescence. Long before her teens, Ethereal became less than charming.

Feather duster badminton came to a halt when the shuttle-cock became self-propelled. As with all babies, the work of caretaking is exponentially more difficult when a child begins to move herself about. A baby with normal gravity scoots, crawls, rolls, and eventually toddles in every possible direction (except up of course) and grandmas, grandpas, parents, and baby sitters must keep a watchful eye. Speed and vigilance are required.

For a typical baby to go up, she must possess climbing skills and ambition. Ethereal possessed neither. Going up came as natural to her as any other direction, more naturally, really. She could scoot, crawl, and roll in any direction: north, south, east, west, and go all those directions on any chosen vertical plane. Down was more difficult but this was not her problem. Coming down was a headache assigned to her caregivers. The little princess would swim through the air and tuck herself among the eaves and insist on a delightful game of "Fetch the Baby."

Anyone who has kept a toddler knows that games do not grow old. Just as a single book can be read three times per night, every night, for three months, the same game can be played a hundred times in two hours and not lose any of its appeal. The whims of a two-year-old are a laborious taskmaster. One who can fly out of reach without a moment's notice borders on the tyrannical. One who on a whim flies out of reach and laughs uncontrollably while you weep and fume because you are desperate for her safety (not to mention the security of your job) is downright oppressive. Needless to say, Nanny Moninne found little help among the other staff once Ethereal developed a mind of her own. Playing with the princess was no longer fun.

When Ethereal reached school age, her parents, though eschewing physicians, did ask their Mandarine ambassador for a consultation on tonal languages. They thought perhaps their daughter's limited emotional range, which consisted of laughing at *everything*, might improve if they could discover perchance that a "hah" had a slightly different meaning than a "ha heh." Perhaps a "ha" starting at a high pitch, swooping low, and ending up even higher might mean happiness with a touch of pensive forethought. But their Chinese guest only smiled shyly and retired, pretending not to understand. He penned a letter to his mother that week with great hilarity, "They think I am magic because I am Asian."

The royal couple then theorized that if meaning could be assigned to different mirthful outbursts, they might slowly stretch their daughter's repertoire. Perhaps Ethereal could be taught that her chortle was slightly sadder than her chuckle and her guffaw set aside for moments of true joy. It was a hope that only desperation could foster. Diction coaches and inflection experts proved expensive and useless, an all-too-common combination.

One day, in desperation, Ita thought of an experiment. Both parents called Ethereal in and, in the most sober tone Ita could muster, she reported to the girl that General Havering had been captured and all his troops cut down by the enemy. Ethereal laughed. This was difficult to take because Havering was a great favorite of the Princess. Her behavior, they thought, was slightly more grounded and sincere in his presence.

The girl was then told that her father's sworn enemy was making haste unabated towards their home. Charts and maps stood by showing the route the enemy was taking. Timetables were laid out and a suitcase was displayed to show how little they could take with them on the run. Ethereal found these facts comical. When next it was reported everyone would have to flee and their palace home would be burned to the ground, Ethereal split her sides. The princess took absolutely *nothing* seriously.

The result of the vain experiment made Ita weep openly. Seeing her mother's tears, the princess commented, "What funny faces mama makes! And water drips from her eyes onto her cheeks! Funny, funny mama!"

This caused her father to lose his temper. He stormed at Ethereal but, in her weightlessness, she floated out of reach, laughing and dancing around him.

"Do it again, papa! More! Such fun! Dear, funny papa!"

She continued to glide from him every time he lunged, not the least afraid, thinking it was a game not to be caught. Backwards, forwards, left, and right, like a giant butterfly flitting about, dancing and floating above his head. Fenton's back was thrown out in the process and he wept from pain both emotional and physical in the aftermath.

More than once her parents stole away for private consult

only to look up and see their daughter peering down, quashing all her giggles in two cupped hands. Vain were the reprimands. Useless were their speeches about privacy and the seriousness of parenting. It was all so funny. Ethereal held the upper hand, and foot, and face, and torso.

Everything was up with Ethereal. She made even the court jester loose his spry step. He was caught with his lute in the corner singing a sad tune. (This was counter to his job description and, of course, garnered a bad performance review.) —

> *In her laugh hid no softness*
> *No balancing sorrow underneath*
> *Snigger snicker chuckle chortle*
> *Shine-less eyes, smile-less teeth*

There are worse sins than laughter, but laughter in the face of all situations grows worse than old, and more than disconcerting.

EDUCATION AND EXERCISE

Ethereal was the perfect specimen of a girl who could (seemingly) neither think nor feel. She was ever charming, the tittering life of the party. Her light nature was fast becoming pure heartache to all who loved her.

The chorus of the mournful tune composed by the court jester (renamed temporary court tragedian) went as follows—

> *When a baby laughs, all is right*
> *A baby's soul is very light*
> *But when by mirth a maid's consumed*
> *Jesters sing a mournful tune*

It did not help that he sang in a minor key. Queen Ita nearly broke his lute over his head when she heard it for the first (and last) time.

The queen, like any good mother, blamed herself. She fired the tutors (the ones who had no tenure at least) and took the princess' education into her own capable hands. On the problem that was her daughter, she brought to bear the great weight of her over-educated, over-feeling, over-thinking mind.

Initially there was success. Ethereal learned to read quickly and could memorize in a flash—without flashcards. Original texts were employed in original languages. Like a parrot the student repeated back, noun upon noun, declension upon declension, accent upon accent.

ETHEREAL WOULD PASS her exams and then apply absolutely nothing across disciplines, much less to her everyday life. Ita came close more than once to linking one synapse to another in her daughter's mind, but each time she approached the moment of connection, Ethereal would break, roll into a ball, and quiver with inexplicable happiness. To see the glorious interplay one school subject had with another was dreadfully serious business and this of course was, to the princess, uproarious.

"Computation applies to literature, so it does. Ha, ha!"

"Science is imbedded in my classic novella. He, he!"

"Latin has helped me understand my biology lab. Ho! Ho!"

When Ita then moved on to ponderous philosophy and complex mathematics, Ethereal would echo back the master works, memorize the formulas, and end each lesson positively screeching with laughter. When Ita assigned as recitation the entire *Lamentations of Jeremiah*,[1] Ethereal obediently memorized the book, in the original Hebrew no less. When she began to then translate it, quill in hand, into perfect koine Greek the princess went into undignified contortions—violent hysterics from which she could barely recover. It was all "so funny!" When the queen had passed her entire body of knowledge, every last jot and tittle of her own education, on to her daughter, she had by her efforts produced a well-educated giggling little fool.

Since the princess could not be saved through her intellect, perhaps time in the gym might profit a little. But as frustrating as mental exercise was, the queen's approach to physical exercise proved equally hamstrung. Intellectually spent, the queen dug out the king's old intramural athletic gear. The weights were quickly abandoned, for when Ethereal took them in her hands, her feet flew in the air—slapstick at its finest. Here even the staff could not keep a straight face and the only thing that could make Ethereal's laughing worse was to have company in her mirth.

Running was also preposterous. Ethereal's mode of progression was to make a bound, alight, and attempt to move her feet backwards and forwards. When doing so she usually made little contact with the ground. Sometimes she would imagine she had reached her landing place before she actually had, and her legs would go mad like an over-exaggerated cartoon character. Her limbs took her nowhere, feet a-blur. Then, of course, she would crow like the very spirit of fun. Competition with herself or anyone else was out of the question. To compare one contender to another or one moment of performance with an earlier one was far too serious business. Any sense of competition or comparison was lost on the light-hearted princess.

"But you ran faster than last week."

Shrug.

"I think you are stronger than our best footman."

"Ok."

Ita had approached Ethereal through an attempt to develop her mind. She then approached Ethereal in an attempt to develop her body. As for approaching things spiritual, Ita balked. The queen was a strong believer that one waited for others to ask about holy things. And the princess showed zero interest. So, except for short morning and evening prayers and the blessing of a meal, all catechesis was avoided, as was the chapel.

In exchange for her hard labor, the queen was weighed down and the princess was lighter than ever.

[9]

THREATS AND PROMISES

King Fenton was growing tired, tired of his daughter's lack of real progress and tired of telling his wife what fine progress their daughter was making. When people are exhausted, self-control ebbs to its lowest point. I do not say this to make an excuse for the king's behavior in this chapter, but I do wish the reader to know he was worn out, weary, dog-tired, bone-tired, ready to drop. His patience was on its last legs—fatigued, spent.

Towards the end of the homeschool semester, Fenton was sauntering down the west wing of palace and noticed his wife exiting the school room, shoulders stooped in defeat. She passed by her husband so blinded by her own tears that she did not notice him. The king let her pass quietly. Queenly sorrow was transformed into kingly anger and his blood was boiling when he burst in where his daughter hovered inches above her desk. He grabbed the giddy girl before she had chance to float away, pulled her in, and struck her.

Ethereal did not cry. But her laugh changed so it sounded uncommonly like screaming. Her face looked grave but not a single tear flowed. Her father beat her three times, then checked for any glimmer of wetness upon her eyes or cheeks and found none. Defeated, he turned to leave. Ita had returned. She stood on the threshold.

Fenton turned back again and saw Ethereal floating high, mouth pressed into a the shape of a smile, but none of the three felt any pleasure.

"More lessons, mama?"

Ita shook her head.

Ethereal did not understand her parents' volatile emotions, but she could predict patterns. Every time her father lost his temper, he gave gifts afterward.

"Promise, promise, make me a promise," she sang, looking at the king.

"I dare not. What is it?"

Usually, this is where Ita would intervene. She would keep Fenton from foolishness and Ethereal from more spoiling. But this time she left her husband to his own devices.

"Promise, promise, make me a promise," Ethereal sang once more.

"What is it?"

"Mind, I hold you to your promise."

"I know. I promise."

"I want to be tied to the end of a very long cord and to be flown like a kite. Oh such fun, I will rain lemonade, and hail sugar-plums, and snow whipped-cream, and—and—and—"

The king had promised and it was so. And, in spite of the reason for the frolicking food fight, a good time was had by all involved. The staff took shifts bathing in the streams leading into the lake well into the night and sweet and sticky flowed the outlets for days to come.

WHEN THE QUEEN left the schoolroom a second time, she wandered in a haze, following her plummeting emotions to the lower parts of the palace where she passed hours, unnoticed. The halls were empty, for the staff had rushed to join the great kite-flying, food-throwing giddiness on the front lawn.

Every set of stairs she encountered, Ita took the downward path. She was done in, beat, shattered, wiped out, toilworn. At last, in an unfamiliar corridor, she came to a dead end. Hardly noticing the small arched door to her right, she simply put her forehead against the wall in front of her and moaned. She turned, slumped to a crouching position, and moaned again. There were no more tears to shed.

Now the queen, hoping to be alone, wanting to be alone, found she was not. From the other side of the arched doorway she heard a murmuring—

> *Alice Alice*
> *of the palace*
> *Alice Alice*
> *wanting more*
> *Who are they to act our betters?*
> *Queen's a hussy*
> *King's a bore.*

It sounded like the chanting of a spell. It persisted like the chanting of a spell. Her blood was boiling when she burst in, ready to pummel the chanters with whatever weapon she found to lay her hand on.

In the low-ceilinged room, Ita found a butler she had once rebuffed, a cook she had once corrected, and a shadow disappearing from the room out a window much too small. A gypsy violin lay on the bed and the queen grabbed the bow, raising her arm to strike. Once, the horse-haired stick whistled through the air and left its mark. Twice, bow hair flying, whip now in hand, the queen stung a recalcitrant servant. Thrice, she raised her hand but never brought it down. Her wrist was caught from behind by the strong grip of the king. Her husband had come for her. She turned, buried her face in his sticky, sugar-plum-encrusted, whipped-cream-covered tunic and wept.

"They've come after her even inside our own palace walls."

WHILE MOST RESIDENTS of the palace were splashing and bathing in the lake that night, the queen had the small basement room scoured. It stank of fish and hemp. In the corner a playing card was discovered, the kind used to tell fortunes and play tricks on the perceptions of the desperate.

Ita had not the energy at first to confront nor even dismiss the guilty servants. But after she collected her thoughts and said her prayers she knew it must be done. Yet when she inquired from the chief steward on the cook and butler's whereabouts, he curtly answered that each had found new positions elsewhere. Ita's face conveyed such alarm that he humbly added, "I wrote them references, ma'am, should I have not?"

The queen in her brokenness had allowed the evil to escape and they would surely start mischief again elsewhere, like lighting a candle in the dark only to see the cockroaches scurry away. That night, she breathed a prayer for mercy and fell into a fitful sleep.

10

INTO THE LAKE

Mercy did come in the morning and in an unexpected way. Both parents had noticed that from babyhood, Ethereal never minded a good cleaning and became a calm, almost normal child in the tub. She had an affinity for the water even as she grew and would lurch towards the lake any time she was within twenty meters. The silken strings (for that is how her retinue traveled with her) would grow taut.

Her mother feared not her daughter's drowning but her being blown away. The wind across the wide lake would pick up in unexpected gusts and, except along the edges, there was nothing to anchor on. Cords only let out so long and butterfly nets, even large ones, were of no use.

After their harrowing day of parenting and a wretched night of second-guessing, the desperate king decided to take the family boating. In this Fenton showed the depth of his love, for though his wife was indifferent to water, he found it a terror. He could not swim and had seen a friend drown in his youth. He trembled as he retrieved a rowboat. He trembled when his family got on board. He shook as he rowed, even as his daughter laughed, feet tucked under the opposite seat to keep her anchored. Mother Ita held tightly to her silken line. Ethereal was fascinated by the lake's depth.

"Mama, papa! It's a giant tub!" she chortled joyously.

The princess batted at dragonflies and lurched at the frogs. She rocked the boat port to starboard and just when her father had had enough, just as he reached the middle of the lake and desperately wanted to go back, just as he was beginning to recall how to turn a boat by deeply dipping an oar, Ethereal plunged in. The silken line unreeled like from a fishing pole in her mother's hand.

In a blink, the princess was gone. The royal couple gaped at each other opened-mouthed like the carp below. In sync both drew breath ready to cry out for every servant within ear shot. Both exhaled without a sound, for in that moment Ethereal bobbed to the surface. Nearly fifty meters away she was swimming like a duck, happily spouting water.

In a blink, down the princess dove again. Her dumbstruck parents could see she was fast approaching their little boat. They waited, watchful and confused. Out of the water popped a dainty white left hand which clung to the side of their vessel. Next their child's face beamed upward, so genuinely content she was hard to recognize. Then over the side was heaved, with a strong right arm, stockings and slippers. "Hold my shoes for me please, mama and papa. It's hard to swim properly with them on." And she was gone again.

"She said please," sputtered her mother.

"She cared for her belongings," sighed her father.

As their child broke the stillness of the lake, her parents were content to sit back and watch and wonder. Was it because christening water had worked the spell that immersed in it she also found her only freedom? And so it did seem, for when in water, Ethereal shared the physics of all other princesses. Most pleasing for parents, though, was that she became other than she was on land—more sedate, better behaved, more aware. Namely, she took notice of her own mother and father as people.

So began a long string of outings on the lake. The king's greatest fear became his greatest pleasure. Rain or shine, the three would row out, missing only the days of deepest winter when the ice spread across the entire surface.

Fenton and Ita consoled themselves with the lovely hours of respite. Each did not mention to the other their same secret hope, a hope quickly dashed. Each had thought, for a short window of time, that the water might work a cure. But each time Ethereal left the lake, alas, all was giddiness again. No conversations, some of them profound and beautiful, were retained. No words of instruction were absorbed past the few short hours. Each reentry was starting over.

One summer day, during a moment of peace, enjoying a semblance of familial harmony, Ita turned to her husband whose hands were at rest on the oars, chin resting on his chest. As casually as she could, she asked, "Who is Alice?"

The king, lost in thought, replied, "Isn't that the girl who had the big to-do with a white rabbit and the March Hare?"

"I'm serious, Fenton. Don't you remember?"

Fenton raised his head. His blank stare answered for him.

"The rhyme in the servant's quarters, darling—"

Alice Alice
of the palace
Alice Alice
wanting more

With a single look the king silenced his wife. She knew now she was on serious ground. Then, from under the boat's bow, came the question. "I want to know too, papa. Is that my real name?"

"No darling. Now swim and play. I see a family of ducks that needs tending."

And off she went like a water nymph. The queen sat staring, one eyebrow raised, not in the least satisfied.

"It was an impromptu limerick to satisfy my sister," the king answered, looking around, though no one was in earshot but an elderly catfish.

"Your sister thinks she has the name ..." said the queen after a moment's pondering.

"And I'm beginning to think it is good for her to think so" said her husband so low and serious that she felt they were being watched.

"I am beginning, husband, to think you are right."

Not another word was said between them on the matter, but that evening they held each other close and doubled their prayers.

Though the princess was better behaved and more beautiful the longer she swam, it was clear her passion was the lake. Her life was bound up in the water and her longing for it was insatiable. She desired now to swim alone and to need no one's help to enter the water, for her frolics in the lake to be hers and no one else's.

Oh! If I had my gravity, she thought, I would fly off my bedroom balcony like a long white sea-bird and splash headlong into the wetness. She hugged herself and hummed, imagining the moment. It was the first and (for a long while) only time she wished to be like other people.

11

A PASSERBY

WHIT NEVER USED his real name nor his title when he traveled. And he had traveled a great deal of late. It's what princes did when they were restless.

"Your standards are too high! Don't be so picky," complained his mother.

"Trust me to choose the girl," suggested his father.

He could do neither and was beginning to cultivate the idea that he may have had the soul of a monk. Hermitages were becoming his favorite hideouts, monastics his favorite company. Overall Whit was fine-mannered and handsome, but of both traits he was unaware. His wanderings had made him forget the pampering of his youth.[1]

In his travels Whit had heard of the princess and her gravitational bewitchment. So famous and mysterious was the growing legend of Ethereal that the children of the villages in and around Lagobel skipped rope to the following rhyme—

> *Princess princess float up high*
> *Princess princess cannot cry*
> *Princess Pod or Princess Pea*
> *Is an old maid just like me*
> *Princess princess float up high*
> *Princess princess cannot cry*
> *Princess Pea or Princess Poo*
> *Is an old maid just like you*

Whit unwittingly added a verse in his head as he walked—

> *Princess princess without tears*
> *Without hopes and without fears*
> *Childlike heart and childish mind*
>
> ...

He couldn't finish it. Not because he wasn't a poet at heart, but because he did not know how it would or should end. Besides, the rhymes, both his own and the children's, were fiction to him. He figured the princess was bewitched but never dreamt she would one day bewitch him. What would he do with a woman with no weight? What might she lose next? Tangibility? So Whit made no inquiries about Ethereal. He was happily single with no dreams or aspirations to be a hero.

But wandering hearts make wandering feet and wandering feet sometimes take young men places they do not intend. Having lost his horse months earlier to exhaustion, Whit was traveling by foot. The summer was coming to a close and this particular evening the wild forest was giving way to a more civilized wood. The wood in turn gave way to a rocky path and the rocky path led up to the edge of a lake.

There is nothing more beautiful than a full moon on a

shimmering lake. A full moon was not available but the half moon above was pleasant enough and Whit was not a perfectionist. Besides, the night was warm enough to not fear frost and just crisp enough to rule out mosquitoes. Whit sank into a reverie, or the nearest thing a man can get to one who has not yet experienced the sensation of falling in love.

A sharp noise pierced the darkness and a chill went down his spine. Was that a scream? Something or someone was drowning. Whit tore off his tunic and kicked off his boots and plunged into the unknown lake.

Near the opposite shore the princess was neither drowning nor screaming. She was laughing that same unanchored chortle she coughed up when reprimanded. She was out after hours and crowing, or attempting to, "Silly papa and mama trying to keep me in. Why should I not swim alone at night?"

Whit's powerful stroke closed the distance between them easily. Once he had Ethereal in his grasp he found the usual resistance given by drowning people. The victim was indeed human, and, he surmised, both a woman and a lady, the latter based on the fact that she was attired.[2]

Whit heaved Ethereal out of the water at a place where the bank was low. He then dragged himself ashore breathing hard and expecting to administer first aid of some sort, and perhaps in a space of time to receive gratitude. Instead, a specter rose into the air screaming.

"You rude, indelicate, interfering man!" and then, in her fit of pique, the princess regressed. "Naughty, naughty, naughty!"

Ethereal would have continued her ascent if she had not caught hold of a pine. Whit, though his first impression told him he had rescued a great shrieking loon, realized in a flash he had found the fabled princess. She was no old maid but young and lovely to behold, even wet and raging.

Ethereal was furious. If gravity had been at her disposal, she would've throttled him. Using branches to both steady herself and move up the bank where the prince had scrambled, she came eyes flashing.

The prince stood frozen in place, fascinated. She placed her dainty foot on the ground, barely navigating her grip on the final limb of the pine to the outstretched limb of the prince. He already perceived that she would float away again if not for the death grip on his arm.

"I'll tell papa!" she said through clenched teeth.

He returned her stare, and quietly declared, "No you won't," with a half smile.

One pull and one push and they both knew she would be whisked away by the wind. A current had kicked up and was fast crossing the lake. Its westerly direction would have blown her far from, not towards, the palace. She was unattended and did not pretend otherwise.

A wave of pity nearly bowled the young prince over.

"I did not mean to hurt you, princess."

"Put me back in," she seethed.

"Back in where?"

"The water, you idiot."

"Come then," said the idiot.

An idiot was exactly what was Whit was becoming. All good judgment had left him on the third "naughty!"

Princess Ethereal by necessity clung to Whit as they moved along the bank and Whit, taking advantage of her disorientation, took a more circuitous route. He found her touch delightful in spite of the torrent of verbal abuse he endured. He brought them to a high bank, almost nine meters above the surface of the water. Here he turned to the clinging girl and said in feigned helplessness, "How am I to put you in?"

She did not know but gave no mercy. "Your problem! *You* took me out, put me back."

"Very well," said the prince.

Catching her up in his arms, he sprang with her from the cliff. Ethereal had just time to inhale before the water closed over the pair.

51

12

FALLING UP

WHEN THE TWO swimmers came separately to the surface, Ethereal found she could hardly breathe. Never before had she experienced such a depth of pleasure. The rush was no laughing matter. Enraptured, she hardly noticed Whit bobbing nearby with a wide sheepish grin.

Whit broke her reverie, "How do you like falling in?"

Treading water, she turned. "Falling in? It seemed to me we were going up."

"There was a certain feeling of elevation for me too," Whit conceded but the princess did not hear.

She, considering for the first time a shared experience, queried, "How did *you* like falling in?"

"Falling in with you has been magical."

"Enough of that." answered Ethereal, deciding that shared experiences were overrated.

"But did you *like* it?" asked the prince.

"It was delightful," she sighed. "I've never fallen before."

"I am available to fall in with you any time you would like," said Whit, devotedly.

"That," said the princess remembering her station, "is most decidedly not proper."

Whit had no answer.

Then to his relief, Ethereal stated with quick confidence, "Well, as long as we have fallen in together, let's have a swim."

"With all my heart," breathed the prince, but Ethereal did not hear. The princess had already made a deep dive below.

The next few hours of swimming, and diving, and floating changed the prince forever. The next few hours of swimming, diving, and floating changed the princess until she exited the lake.

"I must go home," she suddenly said.

"But how are you to return?" asked the prince, knowing her limited movement out of the water but not really wanting a solution.

And it was then that the quandary struck the princess—she had masterfully planned how to get into the lake, but had made no plan as to how to get out. How was she to return to her room in the palace? (Short-sightedness is common to those who have not experienced the harsh consequence of a fall or two). If she wanted to come out again alone, her midnight swims must be the utmost secret.

When the princess had a purpose the wheels of her mind spun quickly. When she next spoke to the man beside her in the water, she instructed him in the same tone she would a footman, "Do you see where the rose light is burning? That is the window of my inmost room. Let us swim there silently and when we arrive under the balcony, you shall give me a push in the correct direction. There is no reason why I should not be able to catch hold of the balcony and climb in through the window."

Whit complied with the obedience of a footman but with no pleasure in seeing her go. He was able to hold to the commanded silence until the very end when he hissed, "Will you be in the lake again tomorrow night?"

"But of course!" she responded.

Then, realizing he intended to join her, she stammered, "Perhaps not ..." But finally, dripping and clinging to her balcony, she turned and shrugged, making no commitment either way.

All Whit could think to say at this point was, "Don't tell."

Ethereal's eyes flashed with mischief and the prince realized he had no need to fear exposure. The princess, at least, would not spoil the fun of choosing for herself. There were so few choices for her to make.

Whit swam a lonely path back across the lake and roved along the shore for hours afterward. The princess, on the other hand, fell fast asleep in her chamber no differently than any other night.

After recovering his tunic, boots, and sword, Whit selected a camping spot in the hollow of a tree, providing for himself a bed of withered beech leaves. From his position he could see the flickering of the rose-colored lamp and yet not fear discovery by those who came and went from the palace. He did not sleep much that night, and then, only fitfully, he dreamt of swimming and weightlessness. The moonlight slowly left the face of the lake and the sun rose to kiss the canopy of the forest above. He did not care at all that he was immensely hungry.

[13]

MOON UNDER WAVES

WHIT WOULD HAVE STARVED HAD he not had connections with hermits. They knew he would not intrude into their thoughts and prayers. They shared their humble resources gladly because Whit had provided so often for them. From these quiet men Whit had learned the art of living only in the present moment, indeed a priceless gift. The future was to be thought of, planned for, but not worried over.

The next day the sun shone brilliant hot. Soon Whit longed for the cold water and his cool princess. But he dared not show himself. To do so might steal from him the possibility of a moonlight swim.

That evening, as Whit returned to his watching of the lake, he caught sight of the king and queen docking their boat in the glow of the sunset. The princess, on a silken cord, was being dragged in after them like the reluctant catch of the day.

Servants met them and gathered the princess with fresh towels and dry clothing. Footmen docked the boat and left but the royal couple remained, sitting on the planks, legs dangling over the pier. Their voices were hushed but still carried over the still waters.

"I fear she was out all night. She has found her own way to the lake," said the queen with a tremor.

"You are right, my darling wife," replied Fenton. "But she is not ours. She never did belong to us. This is true of every child but especially of Ethereal."

The queen simply leaned her head against her husband. Her helplessness pervaded her slight frame. Both knew their hours out rowing as a family of three were coming to a close.

The sun set and the moon rose. The lake and all who watched her went silent. The royal couple retired and the palace darkened room by room, save one. It was then Whit saw how his princess left the palace by kite string.

When one wants something badly enough, one plans ahead. Midday Ethereal had affixed a kite string from doorway to dock and now in the moonlight she crept along it hand over hand. From a distance it looked like a sheet of laundry sliding along a low clothesline, but instead of hanging downward, the laundry blew skyward in a strange prevailing updraft. Imagine the maid in the garden hanging the clothes, but instead of hanging high, she stood on her head hanging low. A blackbird would have more access to toes than nose. The line was easy to find and follow right after sunset while many palace lanterns still burned bright. It was nearly impossible to find after midnight when the lake was lit only by moon and stars. But Ethereal had found a way out before (thanks to Whit) and never worried much past her most immediate impulse.

So the princess held onto the long thin line from doorway to dock. The evening was blustery, adding an element of risk, but eventually Ethereal reached the safety of the water. Next to being tethered to her mother, the lake was the safest possible place for her to be.

From the other shore, Whit, seeing that the princess had entered the water, began to sing—

> *Lovely lady of the lake*
> *My soul suffers for your sake*
> *A stream runs in, a stream runs through*
> *Eddies dance from touching you*
>
> *None to follow, none to lead*
> *None can give you what you need*
> *But the water clear and blue*
> *Medicine and balm for you*
>
> *If you'd deign to be my bride*
> *Where on earth would we abide?*
> *I'd build our castle in the sea*
> *Mermaids for your company.*

Before Whit began a fourth verse, the song had brought Ethereal to him.

"You can stop your musical nonsense. Come swim," she said abruptly.

"Would you like a fall, princess?" said the prince, looking down.

"Yes, if you please, prince," said the princess, looking up.

"How do you know I am a prince, princess?" said the prince.

"I am not without education," said the princess.

"Come up then, princess."

"Molon labe,[1] prince," Ethereal said, showing off her Latin.

The prince was too busy being practical to notice foreign language skills. He took off his scarf, belt, and tunic and tied them together to make a long cord. He sent this down the side of the steep bank to catch his Latin fish. Her words were defiant but, for the sake of the promised fall, she was quite willing be caught.

The rock Whit hauled her out upon was much higher than the first diving precipice and the splash from their dual dive was tremendous. The princess was in ecstasy, and their swim was delicious.

EVERY NIGHT for three weeks they met, and dove, and swam in the dark lucid lake, interrupted only once by rolling thunder and a flashing sky. On clear nights the stars shone so deeply in the depths of the water that the prince fancied he was swimming in the firmament instead of a land-locked lake. Perhaps it was the dragon tears, perhaps the company he kept caused the effect, but when he tried to explain his euphoria, Ethereal laughed at him dreadfully. The princess induced his exultation, but she did not share it.

A full moon brought them fresh pleasure. They dove deeper still and turned round to look up at the great light, shimmering and close, trembling and warping through the layers of waves. Here they held hands in silence. Underwater, shrouded and still, there was a closeness that found resonance in Whit's deepest heart. But breaking the surface also broke the bond, each and every time.

Conversing with the princess in water was a vast improvement to conversing on shore. Her laugh while treading the waves was so much kinder and unassuming. It made Whit hope. But both gentleness and modesty left her as soon as she ended a swim and went ashore.

Underwater the prince felt he might speak to her of love but, of course, could not. When both came up to breathe, he knew he should not. Out of water, on land, he dared not. The talk of their fellowship became gibberish as her quiet submerged spirit changed back again to pert self-assurance. What was sweetness in the water became sarcastic on land. And, worst of all, she would begin to laugh.

Whit, for all his hope, sensed that each time she bid him goodnight, she was really looking past him and speaking to the lake.

[14]
A DROP OF DROUGHT

WHIT WAS a young man of discretion. He watched people and learned from their mistakes instead of having to make all the mistakes himself. He trusted his perceptions and they rarely led him down a wrong path. But with Ethereal he was growing blind. A touch of her hand, a phrase, a look, made him see a woman who loved him, or at least was growing to love him. He did not want to believe what a more sober Whit would have been able to see. All of her momentary affections for him were tied to the lake. Whit's idea of their growing relationship was an imagined one. He was a prop in Ethereal's grand play.

The princess was not being manipulative. She *did* like him, but only by association. Whit had a place in Ethereal's universe because he was the man who swam beside her, the man who let her fall in. Had he been unable to swim, had he not enjoyed endless hours in the waves, he would have meant no more than a can of mushrooms in a castle cellar. Whit, who detested mushrooms, would have gathered, boiled, canned, and stacked mushrooms *if* he could have done so in the company of Ethereal. To Whit, swimming in moonlight was grand, but he only did so all hours of the night because of the princess. His love for her took and kept him beneath the waves. On his own, a starlight swim would be weekly and only in warm weather. Appreciation for the reflection of stars and moon on still waters would have pierced his heart with yearning perhaps only yearly.

In short, the prince could not bear the thought of being parted from the princess and the princess could not bear the thought of being parted from the lake. He loved her and enjoyed the lake and she loved the lake and, in her own light way, enjoyed him. At first glance, the lady and the lake would seem to have the secure, long-term, enduring relationship while the prince was doomed to long-term frustration. But over-whelming agonies and unparalleled pleasures are often over-turned by outside forces.

One night while on a diving expedition, the princess had a sudden suspicion that Lake Lagobel was not as deep as it used to be. She shot to the surface horrified. Without a word, she swam at full speed towards the higher shore. Whit followed, begging for explanation and quite concerned that she might be ill. Ethereal gave him no notice but swam the shoreline giving close inspection but the waning moon did not allow her to come to a clear conclusion. She then swam home in silence, no longer conscious of his company. Whit was left alone and withdrew to his home in the beech tree, perplexed and distressed.

Early the next morning, as soon as she could awaken her staff, the princess dragged her silk ribboned retinue around every shoreline and made mathematical observations. She took precise notation of where the banks were too dry and where plants were withering away. She ordered marks to be made along the shore in all directions, and examined them. Day after day after day the calculating continued, checked and double-checked. At last her fears became a certain fact. The surface of the lake was slowly sinking.

Ethereal went hysterical, her face frenzied, and her behavior manic. The work of marking measurements and calculating angles drove her to exhaustion. She wrote complex story problems regarding runoff, watersheds, and average rainfall. She demanded figures be computed and compared against evaporation and soil absorption. She ordered her staff to solve each complexity, and no one would be dismissed until all found the same sum, or product, or remainder. She threatened to withhold food and sleep if they failed. In a short span, the king and queen intervened and staff was reassigned.

Ethereal wandered the edge of the lake with her mother. That which she loved lay dying before her eyes. The tops of rocks that had never been seen before began to appear, drying in the sun. The princess shook in terror to think of the mud that would soon lie baking and festering. Lovely creatures would be dying, and creatures of the swamp coming to life. As the lake sank, slowly vanishing, the princess began to pine away. Those at court whispered that she would not live an hour after the lake was gone.

She was watching the unmaking of her world.

But she never cried.

[15]

UNDERNEATH IT ALL

A PROCLAMATION WAS MADE to all the kingdom: "Hear ye! Hear ye! Whosoever should discover the cause of the lake level lowering shall be rewarded after a royal fashion!" (hashtag pass it on). Physicians, meteorologists, herpetologists, environmentalists, geologists, speech pathologists, and even Mandarine ambassadors applied themselves. Someone suggested consulting a fortune teller, but the queen gave such a withering stare that the whole courtroom came to a standstill. The suggestion was not breathed again.

Aunt Vespa, of course, was at the root of the mischief. When she heard that her niece found great pleasure in the lake, and understood that by its waters the royal family found moments of respite, she was greatly displeased. When spies brought rumors of midnight swims shared by Ethereal and a "friend," Vespa went into a rage. She cursed herself for her lack of foresight. "By water the spell was made," she muttered, "of course water might make way for its undoing."

For Vespa causing pain was no longer about revenge. She could not stand to lose the company of other unhappy people

63

in her unhappy world. First she pouted, which confused her cat. Then she screeched, which set the feline on edge. Then she doubled over cackling with intense pleasure. And by this the cat knew there was a plan. He purred contentedly.

Vespa caught her breath and stood upright. She crossed the room to an old chest tall enough to bruise shins in the dark, wide enough to hide a body, but long enough only for the body of a dwarf. From it she removed a set of rusty keys and a single opalescent scale that shimmered slightly if placed adjacent to candlelight. The keys she dropped into the pocket of her woolen robe. The leathery shard of skin she clenched tightly in her right fist.

Over a pile of ashes in the hearth hung a bronze caldron. It was cold, dangerously so. Vespa lowered her arm making contact only with the tepid water. Once, twice, thrice she stirred, her bare arm submerged. The water swirled as if it had been wound like a top, pent-up energy driving it at a dizzying rate. In a flash, Vespa released the scale and withdrew like one bitten. Taking three steps back, she muttered three words three times.[1] The water's motion sped on.

Vespa dried her arm thoroughly before reaching into her pocket. Clattering and shaking in her hand were forty rusty keys. Each she carefully oiled, one by one, taking great care as if caressing a small child. As she removed the final speck of rust on the final key, out from the caldron came a head. Following the head slithered eight meters of reptile. The old princess did not look round as the iridescent serpent flowed out from the hearth, slithering back and forth, undulating slow-motion in her direction. She held stock still as it slithered up the back of her stool and came to rest its head on her shoulder giving a low hiss directly into her right ear. The old woman started but with joy. She drew it to herself and kissed it centimeter by inch, wrapping it around her gnarled body. Nubs where arms and legs might once have been glistened as she caressed them. When all eight meters wrapped round, Vespa's right arm was pinned but her left hand was free and by it she clutched the key ring. Woman and reptile as one made their way down steep narrow stairs to the cellar. Or I should say, *a* cellar. As we shall see, there are many more than one.

The cellars below Vespa's little hovel of a hut were layered on top of one another, but overlapped only in part. Each had two doors, one on the east and one on the west. To understand why they were layered thus requires an explanation that would send even the most avid readers into a deep sleep. For our present story, you only need know that one traveled deeper in an easterly direction and traveling back to the shallows took one west. Rarely did one access all cellars in one day, let alone in the very same hour as Vespa was about to do.

Entering the first cellar, Vespa stooped, muttered a magical word, and wrote a musical rune in chalk on the exact center of the floor. Backing up a single large step, she locked the door behind her. Then, careful to avoid all contact with the rune, Vespa descended a few steps and unlocked the second cellar door. The serpent grew heavier.

Entering the second cellar, Vespa stooped, muttered a magical word, and wrote a musical rune in chalk on the exact center of the floor. Backing up a single large step, she locked the door behind her. Then, careful to avoid all contact with the rune, Vespa descended a few steps and unlocked the third cellar door. The serpent grew heavier.

Entering the third cellar, Vespa stooped, muttered a magical word, and wrote a musical rune in chalk on the exact center of the floor. Backing up a single large step, she locked the door behind her. Then, careful to avoid all contact with the rune, Vespa descended a few steps and unlocked the fourth cellar door. The serpent grew heavier.

Now dear readers, my first listeners were quite young and thoroughly enjoyed this repetition in all its fullness.[2] You can enjoy the full repetition too. Simply go back and insert the proper numerics: fourth, fifth, sixth, seventh, eighth, ninth, tenth, eleventh, twelfth, thirteenth, fourteenth, fifteenth, sixteenth, seventeenth, eighteenth, nineteenth, twentieth, twenty-first, twenty-second, twenty-third, twenty-fourth, twenty-fifth, twenty-sixth, twenty-seventh, twenty-eighth, twenty-ninth, thirtieth, thirty-first, thirty-second, thirty-third, thirty-fourth, thirty-fifth, thirty-sixth, thirty-seventh, thirty-eighth, thirty-ninth, fortieth. (I would have written it out for you, but you know how editors are, accusing writers of finding excuses to make a higher word count).

Vespa did the same set of motions in the same exact way forty times in forty cellars. The only difference was the runes. Each of those were unique (if you paid attention to the accent marks). After the fortieth lock, the old woman entered a vast cave supported by forty colossal stalagmites. The cave was directly underneath Lake Lagobel.

When the last key had been placed in the last lock, Vespa could barely move from the weight of the reptile. With the last of her strength, she untwined the serpent from her body and gave the tip of its tail a flick with her strong middle finger. It was several hours before she regained consciousness.

The hideous reptilian creature began to move in slow oscillating motions around the cavern, ever looking upward. First along the edges he crawled, circling ever tighter, eyes fixated, methodically combing every inch of the rocky canopy. As a predator hunts for elusive prey, one chance to strike and no more, the reptile coiled at last, and with sudden explosiveness shot out latching its wide mouth to a small stone protruding overhead. He hung motionless for several minutes, his long body hanging like a chrysalis. Then he began to suck like a naked mole rat hanging from a furless teat, like an overgrown anacondic-leech, like a tick whose belly grows taut engorged on the blood of its host.[3]

Aunt Vespa woke with a start, cried in delight, and rushed to the door clutching her keys in terror. Unlocking door number forty, she rushed through the chamber, her long robe erasing the chalky rune. Adroitly, she stuck a quickly rusting key in lock thirty-nine. Unlocking door number thirty-nine, she rushed through the chamber, her long robe erasing the chalky rune. Adroitly, she stuck a quickly rusting key in lock thirty-eight. Unlocking door number thirty-eight, she rushed through the chamber, her long robe erasing the chalky rune. Adroitly, she stuck a quickly rusting key in lock thirty-seven.

With the disappearance of each rune, a low note sounded and did not cease. Each tone built on top of the next in a magnificent dissonance. Each note pushed Vespa onward, building and building a wall of sound so that when the fortieth and final door flew open, she was lifted and thrown into the dirt, face down in her own small hovel of a hut. Her cat, glad of her wicked company, curled up and slept in the small of her back.

The echo of the great noise did not fade until the sun rose in the morning. The cat was first to rise.

16

EXITS AND ENTRANCES

No HUMAN but Vespa knew of the serpent draining the lake. But the streams knew, and refused to flow any longer in the direction of Lagobel. A song of mourning covered the land, understood in full only by the cicadas—

> *Every spring has ceased to throb*
> *The pulse of fountains dies away*
> *Mountains show not silvery streaks*
> *Running down to find the bay*
> *Crackling courses, thirsty clay*
> *Drought and dying fulfill fears*
> *Hush the falling water stills*
> *None to spare for making tears.*

The king, the queen, and the the prince each loved Ethereal but agonized over her in self-made solitude.

Whit at first tried faithfully to wait for Ethereal to come to him. He followed his old pattern of sleeping most of the day and going to the water's edge at night. He sat and sang what he had written weeks ago for his beloved—

> *Lovely lady of the lake*
> *My soul suffers for your sake*
> *A stream runs in, a stream runs through ...*

He could not continue. There was not enough water left to bring his princess to him. No streams ran in, nor through, nor under, nor at all. He tried to learn the song of the cicada but it was pitched all wrong for his baritone.

Whit finally took leave and sought solace with a nearby hermit. And, when solace was not given, he tried to find answers. The hermit did not give answers. But he did listen as Whit wrestled with whether the lake was dying because the lady had forsaken it, or whether the lady was dying because the lake had forsaken her. Finally, Whit found a course of action. He would go to the palace, remain close to the dying and, if need be, learn to mourn.

The prince exchanged clothing with his solitary friend. Days before he had ceased to shave and his hair had become unkempt in his grief. In this state, Whit presented himself to the palace staff asking only to polish boots in exchange for bread. His terms were accepted.

Just as Whit was making his way in the back door of the palace, King Fenton was on his way out the front. Though the sovereign's heart was breaking, his face was brave. Hand-picked servants, his finest tunic, his best horse, his treasured weapons, and most of his gold were traveling with him. He was on a quest and cared not the cost.

The king's remaining hope was to find another body of water so beautiful it might recapture his daughter's heart and revive what little soul she had. In truth, he went for love of wife. His daughter, he believed, was past saving. Her life was no life, light and loveless. But his wife's soul was bound up in the girl just as the girl's soul was bound up in the lake.

The king remembered his grandfather's stories—how Lagobel had been founded three generations earlier through cunning and valor. Beautiful bodies of water had to be ripped from the grip of great dragons. He wished he was on good terms with his sister, for Vespa held to the lore of their fathers, her fascination bordering on obsession. All he had was a scrap of a memory tied to a scrap of a dragon. A large iridescent scale had been mounted and framed in some anteroom of the palace, but it had disappeared with his childhood long ago. He thought of stopping by Vespa's hovel of a hut in hopes of gaining a single scrap that might prove helpful. Bearing up under a barrage of parenting advice would be a small price to pay if it would save his only child.

But the king did not pause his quest to see his sister, and that was just as well.

The king had kissed his wife but had not said goodbye. Ita had taken to bed in the room next to their daughter, neither woman able to stand unaided. Queen Ita did not know her husband's errand and expected he would join her that night again to warm her shaking body.

At first in her delirium, Ita heard nothing, not even the sound of a new servant scuffling his way through the halls, collecting shoes. Whit had joined the staff to be near his beloved, but all he received of Ethereal was her footwear. He collected her boots and slippers daily even though, unlike the mud encrusted clogs, cleats, loafers, sandals, wing-tips, and moccasins of the rest of the residents, the princess's shoes were never dirty. Footwear that rarely touches the ground never tastes mud. This was especially true now that she kept to her room, curtains drawn to shut out the dying lake. As for the man who swam beside her night after night, she had forgotten him. She had forgotten also her father and mother.

The lake went on sinking. Broad patches of mud widened and spread, fish floundered and eels swarmed. People walked where footprints never pressed before, looking for something of nourishment, adjusting their diets to the rapidly changing ecosystem. In addition to slimy bottom-dwellers they also collected items of value that had dropped from the royal boats weeks, months, and years before.

When only a few of the deepest pools remained, a party of young boys found themselves on the brink of the last remaining brim-filled basin in the middle of the otherwise dry lake bed. Something shiny called from below. On a double-dog-dare, a boy of eight dove in to retrieve the treasure and what glittered was gold. A great platter gleamed with an etching of a dragon, two wings outstretched, claws in the foreground clutching an open scroll. It required cooperation to lift the prodigious tray from the pool for its great dimensions were meant for carrying the whole carcass of a boar. More than once the treasure nearly slipped out of their hands, as if it desired to return to the depths. Grim, knowing they held something of great import, the young men ferried it to the palace where the queen gave them audience.

Queen Ita, who had forced herself from her bed chamber for the sake of her people, quivered when she saw what the lads had drug in. The great serving dish looked neither old nor new but possessed a mystifying datelessness. The message burned into the golden scroll was read to a crowded throne room—the first clue, perhaps, to undoing a great evil that had befallen the kingdom. On the metallic parchment were these words—

> *Death alone from death can save*
> *Make sacrifice beneath the wave*
> *Can Lagobel libation find?*
> *Life for life exchange in kind*
> *Man in love can stay the flow*
> *Heartbeat stopped can stop the hole*
> *Offered free, no bribe nor threat*
> *No repayment, no regret.*

The enigmatical note puzzled the courtiers but not the Queen. She knew what sacrificial love was. So did the shoeshine boy sitting in the corner.

17

QUEEN AND PRINCE

"THE HOLE MUST BE FOUND and filled," said the baritone voice of the shoeblack. The queen stared out through the crowd and locked eyes with the young man. With a wave of the hand all others in the courtroom were dismissed. Queen Ita was past courtly manners, her daughter lying motionless upstairs.

"And *you* are?"

"A man in love."

"It is nonsense that a perfect stranger should embroil himself in family affairs. Do you understand, stranger, what must be done?"

"If Ethereal is to live, a man must offer himself up to plug the hole in the lake. He must offer himself freely, he must love her, and he must die."

"What do you think to gain, stranger? Don't meddle or waste my time. I'll have your tongue cut out." (Queen Ita had never before given this command but it was the first threat that came to mind. Of late, she was finding herself capable of much she never dared before.)

Whit was unmoved. "I am no stranger. I know your daughter well."

"How? She gives no one but herself a second thought. Does she even know your name?"

"She knows me as the man in the lake. She would not know me apart from it.

"That is not love. You are but a water toy."

"I did not say, your highness, that she loved me. Only that I loved her."

"Love the princess? Men do not love for nothing in return."

"I have gained beyond measure. She will die if I don't do it, and life would be nothing to me without her."

"Do not think you are the only one who loves Ethereal. Another stands ready who has loved her longer than you."

The prince was shocked that he had company. Another suitor? But in the next short space of silence, he realized the queen referred to herself.

Still he was at a loss. He had come to die and could not fathom a woman dying, even driven by maternal love, in what he knew to be his rightful place. But Queen Ita was a formidable opponent. Desperate, Whit grasped at semantics.

"The message clearly says 'man,' your majesty. *Man* in love must stay the flow. You love as only a mother can, and with that I cannot compete. But you do not qualify, as unfair as it may seem, due to gender. I did not write the note and we must be careful to follow it. There are no second chances when undoing evil spells."

"*Man*," returned the queen, pointing to the scroll, "in this case, as in many others, is referring to mankind, my young suitor. The female is not excluded simply because she is not explicitly mentioned."

The prince had no answer.

The queen raised her face to the ceiling and then down again in a furrowed stare, "You are mad."

Whit countered, "Yes, I am volunteering to be drowned by inches. That is madness. But to do so in order that the beauty of a moonlit lake can once again be home to the beauty of your moonlit daughter ..."

He then trailed off, embarrassed at the privateness of what he revealed.

"I sang to her, your highness, every night for weeks and she came to me again and again."

Ita knew the song he spoke of. She had sat on the balcony many of those moonlit nights, not seeing but hearing. The tune had given her moments of comfort and slivers of hope. In a low slow alto Queen Ita now hummed a bar. Whit met her gaze and in a slow, low baritone he sang the first couplet—

> *Lovely lady of the lake*
> *My soul suffers for your sake*

Then both together sang—

> *A stream runs in, a stream runs through*
> *Eddies dance from touching you*

The queen shut down the moment of music as quickly as it had begun and curtly returned to the business of saving her daughter.

"Would you like to run and see your parents before you make your attempt?"

"No, thank you," said Whit.

"Then I suppose I should send servants at once to find the hole."

"If it please your Majesty, I have a single request to make."

"I'm listening."

"Only this—when I stop the hole, the lake will fill slowly and the waiting to drown will be rather wearisome. I would like Ethereal to keep me company. When the water covers my eyes and I can look at her no more, she may leave me to my fate, forget me, and be happy."

"That seems reasonable."

"Very well. I am ready."

The prince felt strange in his sense of triumph, having just won the right to die. He did not know that his victory had not been in the song shared with the queen nor in defending the gender-specific narrowness of the etching. He could not have known the secret the queen held close. Ethereal was to have a sibling. And Ita knew she had no right to choose death, even a noble death, for two.

On Ita's order, the bed of the lake was thoroughly examined and the hole was discovered. It was in the exact center of a stone in the floor of the very pool where the golden platter had been found. The pool was now only knee deep, the hole knee wide. A man's leg could act as plug and a man's leg was soon put in. The last few gallons of the once grand and beautiful Lagobel lake would not escape into the mouth of the serpent below.

18

LADY OF THE LAKE

WHILE THE LAKE was being searched, Whit returned to his companion the hermit, and reclaimed his princely attire. He trimmed his hair and clipped his beard then bowed low to his host. After he said his final farewell, he asked that prayers for the dying might be offered. The hermit, re-robed in his peasant garb, nodded twice and blinked once as surety.

While Whit was dressing for his meeting with death, Ethereal was dressing for a joyful reunion with her beloved lake. She was so transported when she heard that a man had offered to die for her that, as feeble as she was, she floated off the bed, bumping her head against the ceiling in ecstasy.

In two hours time the princess was dressed, packed, and ready. She was placed in a small skiff, fastened in with silken ribbons, and carried towards the shore. Upon seeing dry bed as far as the eye could see, she shrieked, and covered her face with both hands. Servants bore the little boat containing the shuddering princess lightly upon their shoulders out to the pool where, minutes before, Whit had lowered his right leg down into the hole. Down he pushed it until the limb stuck fast right below the kneecap. The drain was plugged.

The princess lay on cushions. Wines and fruits, biscuits and bread lay beside her. A canopy was anchored in the mud as shelter. Once settled, Ethereal ordered her servants home. They went without a word.

"They told me you were a shoeshine boy," said the princess.

"So I am," said Whit.

She did not argue but sighed, then asked with an air of indifference, "What happens next?"

"I do not know," Whit replied. "The platter offered no further instructions."

Now the prince sighed. His leg had grown numb. He thought of the song of the cicadas, cicadas long dead. Their crusty shells now lined the bank where they once sat singing. He turned their tune around in his head and adjusted for his baritone—

> *Every spring gone dry break forth*
> *Pulse of fountains flow my way*
> *Mountains loose your silvery streaks*
> *Come to me and with me stay*
> *Fog and fountain, mist and dew*
> *Drought be done there's naught to fear*
> *Break forth O mighty cataract*
> *Drown me in your held-back tears.*

Within minutes a little wave flowed under the boat where the princess lay and continued on its way, splashing up against the Whit's thighs. The keel settled again in the mud and the princess said,

"Sing again, prince. It makes the wait less tedious."

But the prince was overcome. He could sing no more, and a

long pause followed. At last the princess spoke, as she lay back in the boat, eyes shut.

"You are kind to do this for the sake of the kingdom, Prince."

"I do not offer myself for the sake of the kingdom, Princess," answered the prince.

A wavelet, and then another flowed under the boat, and wetted both of the prince's hips, but he did not speak or move. Again the princess spoke, as she lay back in the boat, eyes open now.

"You are kind to do this for the sake of the lake, Prince."

"I do not offer myself for the sake of the lake, Princess," answered the prince.

A wave, and another, and another flowed under the boat, and wetted the prince's waist; but he did not speak or move. Two ... three ... four hours passed, the princess apparently asleep. Finally she spoke, sitting up suddenly in the boat.

"You are kind to do this for the sake of ..." and she broke off, "I am afloat! I'm afloat!"

And the little boat was free to move in the water.

"Princess!" said Whit, "Toss me a line."

"Must I stay and watch you?" sighed Ethereal, "I am just beginning to feel my old light self again."

"I was promised your company until the water reached my eyes. It is only just touching my chest."

"Oh, yes, that."

A silken cord was tossed and just in time, for the lake was filling rapidly and the boat was anxious to explore.

"I think I will go to sleep again," yawned the princess. "You are a very good man."

"Just give me, if you please, a glass of wine and a biscuit first," said Whit quietly.

"Gladly for you, Whit," she answered gently, unsure of the words as they left her lips.

Ethereal took wine and biscuit and, due to the rising water and Whit's grip on the cord, leaned over the starboard side and served him from her own hands.

"Why, prince," she said, "You don't look well! You are kind to do this for the sake of ..."

"I offer myself for your sake," finished Whit.

The princess was overcome and gave not answer. As she fed the prince, he began to kiss the tips of her fingers and she did not seem to mind. Ethereal, for the first time in her life, became dutiful, keeping an eye on her charge with such a steadfastness that Whit wondered at the change in her. If he had the strength, he might have sung his own happy requiem.

The sun went down, the moon rose, and the waters rose as well.

"Can we not have a swim?" asked the princess absently. "The lake is almost itself again."

"I shall never swim again," said the prince.

The princess went silent. She had forgotten again the means by which her beloved lake rose. She took her gaze from the water and returned it to Whit. Choosing only the choice pieces, she fed him a fruit then a nut. The moon reached its height and shined full on the face of the dying prince. As the water caressed his neck, Whit asked feebly,

"Will you kiss me, princess?"

"Yes, I will," answered the princess.

The kiss was long and sweet and cold. The prince smiled, deeply content.

He did not speak again and was past eating. The water rose. Ethereal sat and watched. A wave touched Whit's chin. She touched his chin. A rivulet touched his lower lip. She touched his lower lip. A current caressed between his lips. She kissed them one more time. He shut them hard to keep the water out. Ethereal began to feel queasy. When he could only breathe through his nostrils, she began to look about wildly. When the watered covered his nose, she felt fear for the first time. Her eyes shone strange in the moonlight.

When Whit's head fell back and the water closed over, Ethereal gave a shriek and sprang from the boat into Lagobel lake.

[19]

LOST AND FOUND

King Fenton turned back towards home. Not because he had grown afraid of the dragon he had just begun to track, but because a rain came on the likes of which he'd never seen. There was no way for his lake to not be filling under such a great deluge, and no sense in pursuing another home if the home he left was in the process of being restored. The slaying of dragons was not the mission, only a means to an end.

It was hard going, even when he reached familiar territory. Torrents poured and flowed down the mountains and if it were not for outlets into aquifers, the country would have been inundated. In his mind's eye, the king saw the lake full from shore to shore and smiled a small smile with the thought of how this must please his daughter; his soulless, light-headed, wish-he'd-never-had-one daughter. He crossed yet another newly formed brook and stopped panting.

"There's always a price, always a price," cackled a voice not five meters off to the south of his soggy path.

"Who's there!"

An old woman stepped out of the shadows, hooded and hunched.

"And you are?"

"Someone you once loved, but no longer."

"Vespa, this conversation leads nowhere each and every time. Why do you come out to meet me? Surely not to rehash our childhood."

"My power is ebbed away. And now I retreat."

"Go, retreat then. Why slow my advance?"

"I came to give a choice. Choice ... the great burden men seek, and deny themselves when it is in their grasp."

The rain pounded them both. The king remained silent, refusing to be baited.

Vespa was no longer her old self but not quite her new. When she smiled she showed a set of pointed teeth. Her eyes opened and closed with double lids. Her skin was opalescent and gleaming, nails sharp. She hissed when she spoke to the man who continued to call her sister—

> *Run me through*
> *And for you two*
> *All returns as was before*
> *Set me free*
> *Chop the tree*
> *And chance you'll save the lives of more.*

Vespa spread her arms, sleeves billowing, and planted her feet ready for the sword. Fenton looked past her at the great beech in the background, lit up by lightning. Why fell a tree in a storm? He looked down and shook his head. Vespa's rhymes never did make sense until long afterward. He looked up again in time to see his sister spit out a forked tongue at him, mouth gaping. Always a little brother, Fenton stuck his out in return.

The reluctant king lifted his sword and walk towards the beech. He was in no mood for logic or sibling bickering. Where had logic ever taken him and what was one to do with a sister acting like a dragon asking to be slain? Besides, as crazy as it sounded, the tree called to him.

Something in him loved the great tree. He was glad the rhyme did not call for its felling. The king gave a single half-hearted chop, the very letter of the law. A low large limb dragging in the water broke off, almost leaping in on its own. Deadwood, held too tightly and too long, floated downstream towards the quickly filling lake.

Deed done, Fenton turned back and found his sister gone.

"Spirited away most likely," he told himself. "She's always been flighty."

The king then considered how far he was from sitting in his counting house enumerating coin.

"Damn if I'm not lost in the miserable end of a fairy story," he muttered. "Tolkien and Lewis make it out to be much more enchanting than it actually is."

When Ethereal jumped overboard, she was no longer her old self but not quite her new. Love made her brave and self-forgetful for the first time, but she was inexperienced in these matters. With most of her strength she reached down and wrested Whit's leg free from the terrible drain. With the rest of her strength she had intended to drag his unconscious body to the surface.

But newly found empathy does not counter newly found gravity. For the first time in Ethereal's life, she sank. For the first time in her life, she despaired. For the first time in her life, she unwittingly dragged another downward. And lastly, for the first time in her life, she wished she could trade her life for the life of another. With this final wish, she joined her prince in unconsciousness.

On the landing-stairs of the palace, servants were gathered wringing their hands. Moninne stood crossing herself. They had all heard that terrible shriek. They had all heard the great splash. They were all now listening to a terrible silence. The lake was full again and smooth as glass. Nothing broke its surface but small turtles, dragonflies and frogs. Then came floating something large and ominous like a great carcass half submerged, legs tipped up, great feet clawing to recover.

Moninne could only half swim but could stand the suspense no longer. She threw herself in the lake and paddled awkwardly out towards the mysterious hulking mass, ten servants following in quick succession, breaking the stillness in a great splashing chaos.

In the end, a great beech limb was dragged to shore. Entangled in its branches were two souls, fingers and limbs laced together like the bough that carried them. After great effort by all, both were carried in and placed near a roaring fire.

At midnight, when the landing was vacated and the palace residents were fast asleep (besides two dutiful attendants), a group of stable boys dragged the beech wood to a cove behind the chapel. Here it was sure to be spared from palace fireplaces. The future of the golden wood lay in the hands of master carvers, not hatchet men.

A DOCTOR WAS NEVER CALLED for. The old wise women of the palace knew their business. At first there was not much success. Hope and fear ran together. Patients so long in the water were usually brought in dead, but the night was an enchanted one and enchantments work both ill and good.

At last, early on the eighth day, the princess opened her eyes just in time to see the sun peek through the last storm clouds. Nanny Moninne had joyfully coaxed but three mouthfuls of broth down her. Then Ethereal caught sight of the bed next to hers, burst into tears, rolled over, and fell to the floor. There she lay for hours crying out all the pent-up tears of her life. She cried for her mother's pain and her father's anguish. She cried for the stories she read which had not before moved her. She cried for the Lamentations of Jeremiah and Romeo and Juliet.

When her sorrow abated (and thankfully Moninne had been sneaking in spoonfuls between sobs), she was ready to get up but found she could not. Any attempt at standing landed her crumpled again mid-room.

"My darling child has found her gravity!" sniffled Moninne happily.

"Oh, that's what all the fuss is over, is it?" said the princess, her face in the carpet. "So far, I hate it."

After many efforts, and with help, Ethereal was on her feet, but she had all the ability of a toddler taking her first steps and staggered about like a sailor without sea legs.

During one of these face-to-carpet falls, an attempt was made, for propriety's sake, to carry Whit on a stretcher from the room. But Ethereal, ever watchful, would have none of it. With the queen's tacit approval, separating the pair was not attempted again. They would heal together or not at all.

It was suggested to the princess more than once that a swim or boat ride on the lake would cheer her, but she was not interested. She only grew more irritable with each invitation. Eventually a servant selling its therapeutic properties was told (and I quote), "Go drown yourself." From this harshness Ethereal quickly repented saying, "This gravity ... I feel as if I am being crushed to pieces. It is most unpleasant," then added, "I cannot enjoy the lake until Whit can. Please understand." Word spread and no one asked again.

At last there was movement from the other bed. The prince spoke, barely audible, "If you are well, princess, so am I." Ethereal toddled over as fast as her wobbly legs would take her and pressed her cheek against his, Moninne barely restraining her from climbing in beside him for joy.

"How is the lake?" whispered Whit.

"Brimful," whispered Ethereal.

"Then we are all happy."

"That we are indeed!" answered the princess, sobbing.

Assured Whit would not be moved out from under her watchful eye, Ethereal, on Moninne's arm, wobbled down the hall to see her parents. Both had been in bed themselves in much need of nursing. The royal couple had never followed the tradition of separate bedrooms. Their arranged marriage had quickly become a love match (a fascinating but long backstory).

Queen Ita showed her eldest the mound that was now her belly and Ethereal's eyes widened in surprise and delight.

"It seems, mama, that some lessons were held back."

"Yes, darling. But now you are ready for the weight of them."

She turned to her father who was recovering from travels and travails in the wind and rain.

"Papa, when might we be officially betrothed? He is a prince you know, not that pedigree matters much at this point."

"As soon as you are able, daughter, to walk with any dignity down the length of a chapel aisle," replied her father with a wink.

"Sooner than you think then, papa. Since I will have yours and then Whit's arm to lean upon." she said giving a wink of her own.

Then the king asked, in a more serious tone, "How are you truly, daughter, with your new sense of self in the world?"

"Gravity is overrated, papa, I was a great deal more comfortable without it."

"Ah, comfort ..." sighed her father, as he turned on his pillow and fell fast asleep.

Papa was asleep but Whit had just awakened from a long nap. He motioned for Ethereal to come close.

"I do not know your true name, my darling. To call you Ethereal still when you are anything but ..." his brow furrowed. "I heard a rumor that your name is actually Alice."

The princess shook her head. "An ugly rumor," she said with a half-smile. "And, I do not know your true name either, my prince."

Both sat silently. Both fell asleep and were for several hours in complete unison with the old couple down the hall. True names would wait until the day of their wedding where they heard them for the first time imbedded in the vows. But they did not speak them for themselves to each other until, as a married couple, they walked hand-in-hand along the shore of a brimful lake. A light wind blew across the top of otherwise still waters.

At the exact same spot where they had first fallen in together and with great delight on the count of three, they jumped in screaming true names at the top of their lungs. The splash they made was indeed much greater than the first, having almost twice the gravity.

By the way, the lake never sank again so much as an inch until an incident involving the couple's great-great-grandson. But that is another story.

NOTES

FOREWORD

1. I refer to the original and noble Old MacDonald, not the one made famous by the animal-sounds-make-a-mother-crazy nursery song.

CHAPTER 2

1. Not her given name but she never liked being called Mary Ellen which broke her mother's heart.
2. A word about the rules of succession: in Lagobel, women could inherit the throne if they behaved themselves and married properly. Vespa (Mary Ellen) had married well enough (though her husband had mysteriously disappeared, whether to a monastery or elsewhere is not known) but she never did behave.
3. All royal personages were to send and receive matters of lasting import in the format of an octave (rhyming abbaabba) followed by a sestet (rhyming cdcdcd). Vespa's father should have begun thus—

   When I do ponder most my kingdom's name
   And behold my pitiful few progeny
   That only single son was born to me
   I wonder at the future of my fame
   And as to whom enthroned should next round reign
   And power of wit to genders both the same
   I think the safety of our family tree
   Still lies tradition bond to one like me
   The son the future tumult does best tame.

   I will spare you the sestet that might have followed. It was showy and repetitive, communicating nothing of import.
4. All that saved the princess from complete destruction was that mother and father had not agreed upon a name. Names are powerful things and Vespa had none to work with. Ethereal, a nickname, followed the baby for the next seventeen years. Only the priest knew her true name. Good priests keep secrets, and thankfully, this one was good.

CHAPTER 4

1. A last note about Tannoch—I think her fervent prayers in her new vocation had a great deal to do with the future happiness of the princess. But she does not like me to speak of these things which is the way of the nobler of nuns. So I will say no more.

CHAPTER 6

1. There are magical reasons for this differential but they are outside the bounds of this story.

CHAPTER 8

1. This Old Testament book holds more sorrow than infidelity, serial love triangles, pet abuse, and drug addiction rolled into one.

CHAPTER 11

1. If Ethereal were allowed a chance to wander about in her own adventures, she would have been better off. Getting in and out of scrapes by one's own wits brings about a certain gravity.
2. Most people of the coarser classes did not bother with clothing of any sort when taking a midnight swim, unless of course, it was laundry night.

CHAPTER 13

1. Come and take me. (This sounds much more feisty when spoken by a Spartan during time of war).

CHAPTER 15

1. These words should not be repeated, much less written.
2. As did my aged fourth cousin who has taken to the nickname Snicket.
3. Forgive me for mixing my metaphors. I do not mean to make light of a dark and deadly situation. But honest to God I could not choose between the chrysalis, mole rat, leech, or tick. There are no words to describe this super-creepy event. I am still in therapy.

VOL. II IN LIGHT OF THE NEW MOON

CONTENTS

There is more to a princess than stunning looks, soprano pipes, and an inherent tenderness towards all creation. There is more to freeing a king's daughter from a curse than riding up singing, lips puckered. Fairy stories often leave out the hard parts. True love is a complicated business and for this there is not always an evil stepmother to blame.

Rarely is a princess, if truth be told, a hapless victim—even when a curse falls upon her as early as infancy. And rarely do princes appear out of thin air to rescue distressed damsels. Brave deeds are most always the culmination of many smaller ones and many princes lack follow-through. Complicating the matter even further is the hard fact that not all princesses want to be rescued. Some prefer the charmed life for reasons I will not attempt to explain here.

So what makes a prince set out from the comfort of his castle and persevere? How does he know a damsel is genuinely in need? What kind of damsel can actually be rescued? Perhaps instead of "Once upon a time in a far away land … ," we start with "Once upon a time there was a prince who had no idea he would fall in love with a bewitched princess."

To tell this tale I have again borrowed from George MacDonald. In *The Light Princess*, I stole his entire recipe, though I spiced it up. This time, the recipe is my own but MacDonald provided key ingredients. Those who know his work will recognize a section out of *The Back of the North Wind*, parts of *The Wise Woman*, and a single paragraph from *The Carasoyn*. I think, cobbled together, the stray ingredients go down smoothly. I also believe they have lost none of their sustenance.

I could not cobble a title. Somehow *The Back of the Wise Woman's Carasoyn* is misleading. I hope you enjoy *In Light of the New Moon*.

Sincerely,

A. J. Prufrock

WHEN THE OLD MAN DIED

King Hasselberry of Morganstow did not speak of death, especially his own. His grandson, Caedmon, would sit at the foot of his sickbed, longing to say something of a goodbye. He was always shushed. The topic of dying was not polite conversation when ladies were present and one lady in particular was always present. Aunt Eliza was ever at the king's elbow to care for and cheer. She would pat his wrinkled hand and say, "Your grandson is so silly, Barry. Of course you are getting better." Sweet, charming, Eliza, whom the whole palace adored, had helped the king forget the sorrow of grandmother's passing and had rarely left the old man's side since. Her tender chortle made him feel young. He had stated so but once. Eliza latched on to the compliment and now no one could forget.

Many said sweet Eliza doted on the king because she had no children. Some said she charmed him because she was ambitious. "Silly, ugly, rumors," Caedmon's mother had told him when he expressed concern. "And son," she continued, using all her courage to muster an opinion, "be careful you do not gossip. It will ruin your reputation." She smiled to herself, proud of the hard words she had given. Then, comforting her sixteen-year-old as if he were still a small boy, added, "Your father has the matter in hand." Caedmon's mother felt better after expressing this sentiment but her son, knowing the conversation was over, felt worse. Everyone knew Caedmon's father, Crown Prince Raleigh, was in line for the throne but Aunt Eliza seemed at the center somehow.

Aunt Eliza was married to Uncle Ruprecht, Raleigh's twin. Uncle Rupe had exited the womb four minutes too late to be crown prince and though this fact miffed his wife, Ruprecht did not give a rat's tail for the power of the throne. Uncle Rupe's brain was slow and methodical, processing only wee bits of information at a time, but his heart was gold. He loved his brother's children as his own and idolized Caedmon.

Young prince Caedmon had learned to lean in and listen to the quiet unspoken spaces of palace conversation. Most unsettling to him was that Grandfather agreed with whomever spoke last. Those who pressed close and breathed pleasantries garnered favor. Those who preferred the quiet of the garden were forgotten. Caedmon's father, Raleigh, fell in the latter group. Caedmon would often join his father on these walks across palace grounds and cast about for a way to say what was on his heart, hoping his father would say something of substance. But most walks were silent.

Caedmon enjoyed it when Uncle Rupe joined their strolls. To the pensive, silent striding about Uncle Rupe would add merriment, with Raleigh's children being the main topic of conversation. The subject of wives was altogether avoided—one man having a bride with no opinions and the other wed to a woman who spoke her mind without hesitation. Each twin wondered, with an ignorant hint of envy, what it was like in his brother's shoes.

Once, to Caedmon's surprise and stifled pleasure, Uncle

Rupe broke convention. He let slip that when Eliza brooded about their lack of offspring, she often expressed her frustration by boxing her husband's ears. Raleigh stopped mid-stride and paused. Caedmon watched to see how the moment of honesty might unfold, how this ray of exposure might affect the brotherly bond. The young prince leaned in to listen and learn. Raleigh drew in a long breath, blew a sigh accompanied by a long whistle, and, comforting his forty-year-old twin as if he were still a small boy, tutted, "Thank God, this unfortunate behavior is only displayed in the privacy of your bedchambers. Be patient, she is after all childless. 'Tis a terrible setback to a woman's hopes and dreams." Ruprecht pulled on his beard as he nodded but Caedmon saw the blush on his uncle's cheeks. Older brother by four minutes cleared his throat, turned back to the path with lightness in his step, and commented on the weather. Uncle Rupe trudged heavily, laced his fingers behind his back, and spoke not another word. Caedmon slunk away, hid behind a hedgerow, and cried from an overwhelming sense of helplessness.

Caedmon was helpless to give aid to his Uncle Rupe. He admired the man's persistent cheeriness in spite of Aunt Eliza's private abuse and public charm. Both he and his uncle knew she oozed charm from every pore not just for grandpa Hasselberry but also for dukes, earls, footmen, stablemen, and each and every ambassador who paid a royal visit. But while Ruprecht knew everyone loved Eliza he did not grasp, as Caedmon was beginning to, that everyone was beholden to Aunt Eliza. Poor childless Eliza was behind most every royal favor granted or withheld. She, after all, patted the hand of a lonely king.

Caedmon, sensing his boyhood floated like a barge atop murky undercurrents, pressed the matter upon his mother once more. If he told her of his fear that barnacles attached to the royal vessel were gnawing their way through ever-thinning planks, perhaps he could awaken her womanly intuition, or at least her maternal instincts. Caedmon pointed out plainly that his own future was tied directly to his father's. Upon hearing this sobering reminder, a shadow passed over the queen-in-waiting's face. It was waved off a moment later like a bothersome blackbird. Caedmon was treated once again as a schoolboy receiving a predictable speech on etiquette, tradition, and good breeding. "Remember, my dear eldest," his mother said in a tone so rote Caedmon could mimic it down to the very sing-song note, "Your father's reputation is tied to your behavior. Many eyes watch you. Good comes to the good. Tradition and propriety are our bulwark."

Tradition of course stated Raleigh was in line for the throne, and Caedmon after him, but propriety stated succession was only spoken about by the man *on* the throne. But even when Caedmon could see his grandfather lay dying, no one spoke of dying. Twin sons required clarity and no one clarified. Hasselberry would call for Eliza, she would come and take his hand, and the king would feel he might live forever. But he did not. His last words, "Does everyone still like me?" came out muffled and inarticulate, more like "Dss envy i-fey?" A single salty streak rolled down his wrinkled cheek. Hasselberry was sure he had put out all possible relational fires with the extinguisher of pleasantness. In truth, he had collected enough kindling that the match strike of his death set his kingdom ablaze.

A coup took place. Charm overran tradition and the greater part of the nobility was massacred. The best and brightest fell first, as in most wars, Caedmon's parents and siblings among them. Prince Caedmon had been in the stables when the melee erupted in the palace. He had been about to strip and wash off the smell of horse and hoof but, upon hearing piercing agony followed by eerie silence, he thought better of it. He instead traded his princely attire with that of a stablehand, rolled on the floor of an un-mucked stall, and walked way from his home foul and filthy, leaving his Arabian steed whinnying after him from the paddock. He did not look back. The sacrifice of his mount and all vestiges of royal identity saved his life.

Caedmon, son of Crown Prince Raleigh of Morganstow, had read of princes setting out to do exploits. He told himself this was his case. As he considered the adventure that had been thrust upon him, the only foe he perceived was the ignoble dragon of despair. He, of course, could not see that fighting the biggest beast first put him in good stead for what was to come. All he knew was that his world had come crashing down.

[2]

A WOMAN IN THE WOODS

THE NEIGHBORING KINGDOM of Kirkhampton and a lowly job hid Prince Caedmon from half-hearted pursuers. He found work in the stables not of a duke, nor an earl, nor a baron, nor a bishop. An ordinary farmer offered the wages of room and board and Prince Caedmon gladly accepted.

Caedmon's love for horses had given him practical skills. Even as young prince he demanded his share of saddling, bridling, and brushing, though palace grooms would never let him touch a muck rake. So cleaning stalls was new but the smell was not and the sweetness of horse sweat and hay brought comfort. Picking hooves and scooping feed made him at times yearn after a good gallop but a stableboy did not prance about on his master's steeds, and these were bred for wagon and plow.

Caedmon settled into a small room above the barn and the fellow servants took to calling him Wesley, a character from village lore. A Wesley ditty, changed slightly by each generation, was applied to Caedmon as well—

In the barn sleeps Wesley dear
Out of nowhere did appear
But quiet work is worth its bread
We will not see a stranger dead
Warm your chapped hands by our fire
Kiss the ring of village squire
Clean the stable, gut the fish
May life be just as you wish.

When days off presented themselves, Caedmon, now answering to Wes, wandered the surrounding forest restless, spending a day and a night when nights were free, and only a day if that was all to be had. He pondered the fate of a royal stableboy. His once polished speech was slipping further into servant slang with each passing week. What was to become of the elocution lessons forced upon the son of a crown prince? What was Caedmon to do with high verse in second and third languages? None but the town squire knew how to read and write and that for only rudimentary village transactions. None of the farmhands had held a spoon or fork, much less dined with a full place setting.

The fading manners and odds bits of education blew away like autumn leaves crumbling down, but grief held on, lichen on bark, fall and winter, spring and summer, twice round. Caedmon forgot himself into the Wesley of the song. Except for the fingers in front of him (the endmost knuckle bent slightly inward like his mother's) he would have sunk submissive and resigned himself to forgetfulness. Except for speckles on his forearms (which came with too much sun like those on his father after long hunts behind the hounds) he would have forgotten his grief. He would have drowned it singing tipsy by the fire with the farmer's daughters and sons.

Palace life had taught Wes well to hide feelings, so when

his grief broke through it was when he stood alone. There was none to tell in the stable but the horses. There was none to tell in the forest but the moon.

Each time Wes ventured forth from the measured domestication of Kirkhampton, he pushed further into the wildness of the trees. He wondered if he had what it took to make his inner solitude an outward one as well. The occasional overnight, though he never stayed the same place twice, was no proof. Could he live as a woodsman or would a madness overtake him?

"Where are you going this time, Wes?" the field hands would call out.

"Just a little further," came the answer.

The haunting beauty of the ever-deepening woods kept calling to his weary sadness. And Caedmon, now called Wes, fell into her embrace.

WHETHER THE FORTIETH or fiftieth excursion, Wes lost count. He did remember, when later telling the story to his granddaughter, that the moon was only half full when into his forest reverie came a quiet rustle. Then, bending branches and firm footsteps crescendoed into wild crashing causing him to jolt up, jugular pounding, hammering his head into the low ceiling of his lean-to. A less than princely word hissed through pursed lips and instinctual fear, not felt since his last night in Morganstow, held him stock-still and silent.

Passing nearby in the darkness, so close he could see breath silhouetted on the face of the moon, was a tall shrouded figure clutching smaller one. The smaller, a boy no more than nine, was struggling in fierce terror as loud as choking fright would permit. Wes felt about for his knife. The blade was made for whittling not battle but it was the closest thing to a weapon he possessed.

Groping about to find the hilt, Wes crouched ready to spring when all went silent. The victim had gone limp as if too tired to struggle any longer. The cloaked figure turned, threw back the garment and set the child down. Wes noted the child was unharmed and released his grip on his knife. His eyes flowed upward and saw the face of a woman regal and stately. Her face was ageless and beautiful, fearsome and tender. Her stature seemed to tower over all the royal men and soldiers previously known. Wes did not move, did not breathe, and a new terror displaced the first one, a fear unlike that of Morganstow, an apprehension of unfolding exposure.

Wes glanced back at the boy. The lad squinted through swollen eyelids and cast an unbending look up at the woman's face. She gazed down gravely. The boy was free but did not run. Instead, he rushed at his captor butting with his head like a ram. The folds of the cloak closed and the attacker fell back bruised and dazed like one recoiling from a bronze shield. The boy sat stupefied where he fell until the great lady lifted him once more. He flailed and was set down again, and again twice more, raging, tight-fisted, eyes inflamed. Each time Wes was sure his presence had been discovered, for in each and every round of tantrumming the lad was set down within arm's length of the hiding prince. But the child, consumed completely by fury, knew nothing but the unchangeableness of his foe.

At last ferocity formed words, "Ogress! Ogress! You shall not carry me to your house and make a meal of me!" The defiance came with raised fist and through trembling lips, causing Wes to feel both pity and admiration. And then the little arms fell to the child's sides, spent, and he stood on the path unable to move.

Kind, stern familiarity reached out and took his hand. The

woman glanced not down but simply stood by his side. Together they faced the moon. The wind blew through her garment and she began to hum, then sang soft and low. Wes noted her cape was cashmere and the boy's tremors abated as it brushed up against his tear-stained cheek. The music was lullaby and requiem woven seamlessly against the backdrop of the billowing cloak—

> *Out in these woods*
> *We stand here still*
> *The wind foretells a coming chill*
> *The distant stream says we should go*
> *Let my yes becalm your no*
> *The heart of stone*
> *The weary moon*
> *To think you're someone much too soon.*

But once more tantrum rose, turned, and trampled the melody. Stomping foot and screech pierced the woven beauty, "Sorceress!" cried the child, snatching away his hand, "You are an ugly old woman and I hate you!"

Before the boy's words had finished tumbling forth, the lady had dropped his hand. Before his screech had made its final echo against the trees, she was several steps away down the path. Her pace was steady and she did not look back. As he stood shocked, struck with the first grapplings of the notion that perhaps he was not too precious to be left, the woman vanished away in the dim moonlight. The moon peered down on him, the height of pitiful loneliness.

With the same abruptness with which he cut short her beautiful music, the boy charged after her screaming. A guttural wordlessness called after a woman whose name he had never bothered to ask. The forest was silent except for the pattering of a child's feet and his pleading, "Don't eat me, don't eat me, don't eat me," all the while drawing closer to the one fought against.

Wes moved after them, unsure of the story he had fallen into, but captivated. The gap between the woman and child closed, for the lady had slowed her pace. The boy reached her with his arms raised. She stood bent, waiting to swoop his little body into her great arms. Her cloak folded round and instantly he was asleep.

As the little one began to snore, the woman glanced at Wes with eyes that first invited and then warded off. Wes stepped backward a half dozen paces before turning to go. But even as the distance between the travelers increased, the sound of the woman's song did not fade until the sun broke through the darkness of the trees.

THE NEXT MORNING Caedmon gave notice. The farmer asked only that he stay until a replacement could be found. Two years' faithful labor was more than the man had expected and he was grateful. The farmer's daughter looked up from her plate and sop and blinked back the coming tears.

[3]

THE FOREST GROWS FIERCE

WES'S LONGING TO see the woman again troubled him but did not dampen his determination. He rushed through the close of a workweek, pushed into the forest through tangled branches, and trod upon paths familiar and long-forgotten. He choked on growing jealousy, aggrieved to admit he envied the boy who writhed and fought against the woman's arms, arms he would have fallen into most gladly. He took stock of his own limbs. Legs and torso were long and lean, all signs of childhood had flown from him. His days of being carried were over.

Under the cover of darkness, Wes settled upon a stump too dry for even moss to grow upon. A long stillness asked him a question, "Why would a woman travel with an unwilling child through uninhabited wilderness in the dark of the night?" Loose ends flitted about trying to connect. The wind blew in unpredictable gusts and cricket song answered back. Then all sounds scattered at the noise of approaching footsteps.

The same actors as before approached in scene two of the same play. The grand lady once again set down a miscreant child. His tuft of golden hair glimmered in the moonlight, his countenance dark and glowering. Once again, the boy jerked his hand away from hers as she offered guidance. The woman then took a single step eastward and beckoned. But the boy turned his back and stamped each foot in singular stubbornness and jutted out his lower lip. A long silence settled over the wood and when the child whirled around, he found he was alone.

Shrill agony edged with anger rent the air. Wes made no move and the trees paid no heed. But other creatures awakened with hungry interest. Wes had moved to cover his ears to dampen the high pitch of the boy's bleating but dropped his hands upon feeling the low trembling bass of a rumbling growl. The tantrum cries had called an army of wolves. Two persons, it seemed, were to pay the price for one's folly. A wave of shock grabbed both by the throat as the pack closed in from all quarters.

An old she-wolf shot through the woods honing in on the smaller prey, eyes glowing brighter as she drew near. Terror silenced the child. His mouth opened in a grimace as if he were about to bite instead of suffering the sinking of great fangs. One final leap and the monster would make him her meal. Wes again felt about for his useless knife. Airborne came the she-wolf but, at the height of her arc, she was caught by the throat in an inescapable grip. From behind a great oak the robed woman had thrust a mighty arm and shook the wolf but once before throwing her down senseless.

In an instant the boy was in the woman's arms again, flinging himself into the folds of her cloak as the remaining wolf pack rushed in like the sea. Wes, now high in the arms of the oak, shook among the acorns and leaves. The woman below remained erect, an invincible tower against the crashing breakers of tooth, claw, and yellow eye. Through the ravenous pack she glided, a stately vessel bearing up her charge. Wolves leapt one by one, then dropped, falling back against the next, only to slink away confounded. The tide changed. The forest quieted. The moon shone on above it all.

The woman's pace neither slowed nor quickened but moved along the path illumined by stars a single footprint at a time, the constellations taking turns watching over her steps. Wes shimmied down the oak, not pausing to wonder or question or ponder, determined only to avoid abandonment. He followed hard after, but his tracking skills played no part. He followed in her footsteps because she chose to let him. Not a word was spoken between them.

The moon was still quite high when a whitewashed thatch-covered cottage gleamed in a clearing before all three. The woman set her barefooted burden down on the well-tended grass. Wes stood on the edges with one foot only on the manicured lawn. Glancing about, he noted an invisible wall divided cottage land from the wild wood—no branch overreached, no unplanted vine crept in. Wes remained on the edges and watched.

As soon as he was set down the boy forgot. He forgot the dread of the wolves and remembered only his fear of the woman. Anger awoke and trust fell into a dead sleep. "You did that on purpose!" he screeched, as if her silence rather than his bleating had called the wolf pack forth. Making no answer, the lady moved towards the cottage then turned to address the child, "Loman, you may not come inside my house until you stand at the door and knock and ask respectfully to enter." She disappeared within and little Loman was left alone on the lawn staring at the moon.

The wolves renewed their howling and were soon joined by the hissing of serpents and thrashing of bat wings. A great cacophony swept towards the cottage like a shadow across the forest floor. Fear gripped Loman though not a single malicious creature set foot or paw or scale upon the property. Deciding the ogress was a lesser threat than the creatures encircling him, Loman began to glance about for a door. He darted about each end of the cottage but spied neither knob nor gable nor latch. He rushed the white wall kicking, only to gain a nasty bruise on his right middle toe. He wanted to roar with rage but recalled the army of wolves and silenced himself. He threw himself upon the grass and lay still. And in his stillness Loman heard the stillness of the forest. All had taken on the quiet of the cottage.

The land below the moon mirrored her luminous silence and in Loman awoke real tears—soft, mournful tears of true disappointment. In that space, he wanted to be taken from the loneliness of the night sky and the terrors waiting in the forest. He wanted to see the wise woman again. But how was he to knock when there was no door?

Loman picked up a stone, came towards the cottage, and knocked on the nearest wall.

A voice came saying, "Who is there?"

"Please, old woman, you know it is I," Loman retorted and stamped but once.

Silence was the reply.

Loman then rapped with his bare knuckles.

And voice returned, "Who is there?"

"Loman," came the curt answer.

Again, silence.

Little Loman slapped desperately with the flat of his hand on the cottage wall.

"What do you want?" said the voice.

"Oh, please, let me in! I am afraid of the moon and the wolves in the wood. Please won't you let me in?"

A door opened.

With the turning of the hinge, the youngster threw his arms around the wise woman's shoulders and buried his face into her neck. She gathered the child to herself and, for the moment, his suffering and terror were left outside in the forest. Before she stepped backward over the threshold, and before the door closed behind them for the night, her voice, clear and strong, called out, "Take the beech staff, Prince. It is leaning against the shepherd's hut near the south end of the clearing. You must have it for your return." In those orders Wes was dismissed for the night, and yet called to come again. He was sent away but not abandoned. Dearest to his heart, he knew she knew to whom she called to come back to the cottage in the clearing—not Wes of the stables but Prince Caedmon of Morganstow.

He left with the staff in hand. His pace quickened for he sensed a storm was brewing and remembered giving his word about a mare that needed to be shod. He hardly noticed the journey home or that gathering clouds ringed the moon like the shaven crown of a monk.

[4]

OUT THE BACK GATE

IT WAS some weeks before Wes's replacement came. He was a boy less than twelve but he already knew hard work. With eager ability he learned the ropes and reins, buckets and oats, hooves and whinnies. In four days he was ready and Wes was relieved of duty.

Wes rose early, put the few things he owned in a pouch, and said goodbye to the taciturn farmer. He kissed each horse on its velvety nose and thanked them for their listening ears and discretion. It was neither easy nor hard to leave.

He carried himself in much the same manner as before, as if in a night or two he would return refreshed to fall back half-heartedly into mindless work.

"Where are you going this time, Wes?" the field hands called out.

CAEDMON WAS HALFWAY across the second pasture before he heard footsteps behind, lightly gliding along so as to delay detection. Small feet stepped into the larger prints leading the way, going unnoticed in the shadows of Caedmon's rhythm, step for step, breath for breath, stride for stride, pace for pace. He stopped and his follower froze. He turned to see the farmer's daughter, not yet sixteen. Salt streaks stained her face, making her pretty for the first time. Wes had given her no notice before this moment when they stood face to face in her father's second field.

Caedmon, unpracticed, had no words.

"You are going then for good?" she asked as she stared past him into the dark forest. Caedmon cleared his throat and grunted out a "yes." The sunrise behind him caused the girl to shield her eyes.

He wanted to ask "Why?" for he was truly befuddled by a farm girl following in his footsteps instead savoring her last minutes of precious sleep. A long hard day lay ahead for every resident of the farm.

Caedmon's hand drifted to his chin ready to give aid to his lips and slumbering tongue. The girl's hand drifted upward to twirl a loose strand of her mouse brown hair. Having no plan past staying on his trail, borrowed words bubbled forth, words she once heard whispered in the corner of a tavern, words she did not understand but seemed to have impact. She twisted the lock and looked shyly downward, "If I pleased you somehow, would you stay?"

Caedmon stepped backward but in a few moments recovered. He noted the girl before him trembled even though the air was warm and she wore several layers, every item she owned in fact. How long had she intended on following? He took a deep breath and spoke to her softly, "It's Kassia, right?" She nodded and looked up into his worn face. Glad to have the remembrance of her name as a small token of tenderness, he continued, "There are gifts too precious to offer, Kassia."

Kassia nodded again but he wondered if she had heard his carefully chosen words. Her eyes had not left his face. "If I could only write," she whispered, "I would make you a poem."

"So kind," whispered Caedmon in return, "but the sweetness of your goodbye ...."

"May I give you a kiss?" she broke in.

Caedmon shook his head and Kassia's face fell. A sorrowing sense of lostness too well understood was before him, the sun shining full now on her young face. As the dawn broke over them both, Caedmon held out his left hand, "No kiss, Kassia, but we may travel side by side until I reach the final gate." Her calloused right took his offered left and they strode in silence breathing deeply the crisp morning air.

When the last gate came into view, Kassia struck her sternum with her free left hand where it stuck fast as to stop some hidden wound. Her pace did not slow nor her head turn as she spoke, "I do not understand. My heart screams and my rib cage aches as if a ribbon of fire were weaving itself in and out and through like a shuttle on a weaver's beam."

Continuing forward Caedmon answered, "It will pass. It must pass and you will find the one for you, and he, if he has any sense, will treat you kindly." He had tried to borrow her bravery but his voice cracked like a young adolescent.

But the girl had an inkling of who walked beside her. In spite of the grime, in spite of the lowly work, royal anonymity had worn thin. "You are something more ... I want something more," she said. And Caedmon then knew the timeliness of his parting. He did not answer her but began to sing a ditty from the village common. Kassia joined him on the chorus—

I cannot give you darling more
than hard work done and kisses at the door
Daily bread, dirty boots on the floor
I cannot promise more.

The duo had exhausted all the verses twice by the time they reached the final gate. Turning, Caedmon placed a hand on her shoulder and said, "Do not think what you want, dear Kassia, is foolish just because I cannot provide it for you. You are no fool. Feel no shame for any of your words to me. If you had not followed we could not have shared this walk and it was a thing of beauty. Beauty is never to be regretted."

"Beauty?" Kassia questioned. "I cried the whole way."

"Tears are often beautiful."

Kassia nodded and wiped them away. Caedmon disappeared into the forest, staff in hand.

[5]
PRINCE LOMAN'S LAMENT

THE STAFF in Caedmon's hand was not just for clearing cobwebs woven across the forest path. It was not just to aid and abet his steps on upward climbs. It was also more than a stout weapon against inevitable foes. If its keeper held it upright yet loosely, it leaned and thereby led. If, in the night, its owner stilled his breathing to match his pulse, the staff glowed. There was no rushing its guidance. It led slow, clear, and peaceful—or not at all. In the hot afternoon the staff slept, so Caedmon dozed as well, both leaning their spines against the same great trunk.

Two hours of restful slumber and Caedmon awoke at the sound of human footsteps on dried twigs. He squinted and saw slinking past the very boy who had thrown himself into the waiting motherly arms within the cottage.

Loman now wore new boots, a clean change of clothes, and possessed the look of one well-rested and well-fed. But his slouching cowardice was unchanged, except that it crept in the opposite direction.

Coming abreast, the boy straightened and looked about.

Caedmon remained seated and still. Catching sight of the watching man, Loman's eyes widened in wariness.

"Are you lost?" whispered Caedmon.

The boy shook his head.

"Do you need help?"

Again a shake.

"Is the woman with you?"

A sneer passed over the child's face, twisted and grotesque. "I gave that old hag the slip. She was trying to fatten me up, but I know better."

Caedmon looked on in silence, which, to Loman, was an invitation to continue. The little man puffed up full height and lifted chubby fingers to Caedmon's lips, "You may kiss the royal hand if you wish. I am more than you know. I am a prince." Stone-faced, Prince Caedmon kissed the hand of Prince Loman.

Loman began to strut, "I have just escaped the witch of the woods, one of the few ever to do so." Caedmon raised both eyebrows and gave full attention. Loman, noting his audience was duly impressed, sat himself upon the stump as if enthroned and barreled on in full disclosure. "Not many leave alive from her snares. She captures souls to feed upon, but before she dines, she enslaves."

"How wise and brave you must be," encouraged Caedmon. "Please, young sir, tell me more."

"When you address royalty, my good man, use 'your highness,'" instructed Loman.

"I'm sorry, your highness. Would you please tell me more?"

"She offered me many a fine meal, excellent to sight and smell but full of hidden magic. This witch had in mind that I, a prince, would earn my food, keeping all nourishment out of reach, expecting me to sweep and dust her hut before a single spoonful."

Caedmon kept a serious tone, put his hand to his mouth and gasped, "Were you indeed treated so terribly? I read somewhere once that her cottage was a place of protection from dark forces that linger in the forest."

"Protection from what?" huffed the prince.

Caedmon looked at him, this time only one eye-brow raised.

The boy rushed on, "All that threatens in these woods are mists and echoes. All are designed to drive the weary traveler into the arms of an ogress. I stand here whole, not due to the witch, rather in spite of her."

"I can't imagine, your highness," said Caedmon with sarcasm so obvious he checked himself, "what you must have suffered at her hands." Caedmon's mock empathy was all the invitation the young sovereign needed to inspire a woeful soliloquy.

"I will impart to you, as a kindness, what I have learned through much suffering. I escaped only this morning from the most charming ogress. She found me exhausted and weakened in the midst of an arduous quest."

Here Loman noted Caedmon's puzzled face and paused to educate his audience, "I may seem young but I am first born and they accelerated my training due to my innate abilities." Caedmon nodded and Loman continued. "I was sent to capture or kill the great wolf that hunts on the edge of this forest. Livestock goes missing nightly from our fields. The uncle who sent me was unaware, the bumbling fool, that a witch had cast her spell over the entire wood. She has the power to make one wolf seem like many. I had planned for one enemy, readied my knife for one, honed my bow for one. When dozens appeared I froze in shock and, I am ashamed now to say, feared that I would be overcome. Seeing a cottage, I entered to catch my breath and regroup for the battle outside. But the battle was not without, but within. The enemy inside the cottage feigned to nurture me when my destruction was her desired end."

Here Loman paused for effect. Caedmon leaned forward and widened his eyes to show both surprise and interest. The young prince continued.

"Thinking the cottage empty, I had rushed in. There, by the fire, stood a woman with a warm cup of milk in her hand. She gave me to drink and I foolishly trusted. One sip was enough to send me into a drugged sleep. I awoke to find myself locked in but was determined to resist.

"I refused to speak, eat, or drink. Even when she offered comfort to me in every way most charming, I refused, unwilling even to look her in the eye. I stared only at the fire, pretending I was alone.

"At last she had to take her leave. I suppose even witches must go to market. 'Loman, look at me!' she said, but I would not. 'I am going out.' I paid her no mind. I am not so simple as that. (How she knew my name I do not know. Black arts!)

"'Loman,' she said, 'You must keep the cottage tidy while I am out. Keep the fire bright, the hearth swept, the kettle boiling, the windows clear, and the bed made. After you work, you will be hungry. Open the second cabinet, and you will find a meal.'

"A long list of chores had been set in front of me for the honor of serving myself a single meal. But her controlling impudence had just begun. 'Remember what you have already gone through to reach this house,' she said. 'Do not leave it. This is the safest place for you—in fact the only safe place in all the wood.' But I knew better. Her gentle tone was all facade. She meant to eat me and the stories of surrounding danger were only to frighten me and bind me to her will."

Loman stood now upon the stump bursting with pride. He

continued his speech thumping his own chest. "She left me locked in the silence of a lonely cabin, expecting me to keep her hovel clean. I could tell by her carriage and the gleam in her eye she knew exactly who I was and my station! Perhaps I might have cleaned as a favor, straighten up as I have seen the servants do. But to force me to labor for my bread was an insult of the basest kind. Day after day, I let the dust fall and the bed remain unmade and the hearth unswept. But I grew hungry."

The little prince's hands pressed his abdomen.

"The peasant class fasts because they must and the priest class fasts because they choose to, but royalty must eat. The sharp mind necessary for ruling relies on a full stomach. Still, I withstood my hunger. The food was sure to be enchanted; eating was a step towards enslavement.

"The third night she held me captive, darkness and wind moaned about the cottage. I resisted the comfort of the bed and fell asleep sitting in front of the hearth. My dreams were savage and I awoke to them coming true. Strange cries filled the air. Birds clawed at the windows from all directions, a far greater howling than the wildest wind. Not till the first glimmer of morning did it cease. I cannot tell what would have happened if I had curled up like a chump in the soft bed and not kept watch.

"All that was left of the fire was warm coals nestled in ash. Signs of the onslaught displayed themselves, marks of the animosity nature harbored for the unnatural abode that held me. Windows were covered with feathers and claw marks and bird excrement.

"It was at this juncture I realized, hungry and exhausted, that I had to brave a risk. Escape required strength, and for that I must eat. So I took on the outward form of a servant, calculating (quite correctly, mind you) that I would remain inwardly free if I offered only outward obedience. Pretending full submission to the web of magic that bound me, I threw a heap of pinecones on the dying embers and a flame blazed up cheerily. I caught up a feather duster and wiped every surface, though the dust flew so furiously I nearly choked. I then swept, remembering how the servants of my palace cleansed the marble floor. Next, driven by hunger and willpower, I made the bed.

"Each time I completed a task, I checked the second cupboard. Again and again there was nothing. Not a crumb of sustenance even when not a single speck of ash remained upon the hearth."

Here the little prince paused for empathy and Caedmon did his best to provide. Loman leaned towards his listener as if telling a great secret.

"Get this, the intrusive witch wove the spell so I even had to clean myself! The magic was set so I had to draw my own bath, scrub my own body, brush my own teeth, and comb my own hair. Only then was I rewarded with a loaf of bread and a pitcher of milk—whole wheat and goat's. Not to my taste, but I was determined to survive.

"Strong again on meager rations, I checked about for a way out. Spying a high window latch near the westward door, I pried at it with the handle of a broom. But while I focused on the freedom close at hand, my enemy fell upon me. The door opened slowly and pinned me out of sight behind the oaken panel. The ogress took a few paces in, seemingly pleased with all I had done. A strange look of hope had entered her eyes, but before she could set her bewitching glare upon me, I darted past her and out through the open door."

At this, the boy looked up to Caedmon with a glow of triumph, the face of a dragon slayer. So pleased was he with himself that he bowed low, expecting applause.

The little prince straightened and eyed his silent listener, sizing him up. He then stepped down from the stump, hand clasped behind him, and circled around his listener assessing. Loman rose and stood to show his full height. He cleared his throat and commanded, "You shall be my valet. Accompany me safely to the palace in Flintroy and I will see you are properly rewarded. If all goes well, I will take you into my service."

"No thank you, your highness," Caedmon returned. He stifled a laugh, for the boy was dead serious, acting as both nurture and nature had formed him.

Loman's eyes bulged and, in a flash, on came the fit, out came the fangs, towards Caedmon flew the feet and fists. But Caedmon, having seen these passions twice already, was prepared. The urchin was held at safe distance by the ready staff.

"We ... " said Caedmon, steadying the weapon against the flailing force, "are ... going ... different directions, I'm afraid."

"You are a mooncalf chowderheaded dingbat of a fool!" screamed his would-be assailant, stringing together the strongest curse words he could muster. "You will be sorry when I am king!"

Worn out by his own outburst, the boy at last skulked on towards the south. The staff was awake again in Caedmon's hand and leaning east. The two parted and Caedmon hoped to never see him again.

The wolves began again to howl, this time a little more hungrily.

[6]

CAEDMON AT THE COTTAGE

BY THE TIME Caedmon reached the cottage, the sun was setting. He did not hesitate, as he later would, to enjoy the manicured beauty, but with confident strides walked straight up to the front door. The door was bright and red and welcoming, making him wonder why Loman had faltered so weeks before to find entrance. He paused upon the stoop and gently knocked with open palm. The door was unlatched and opened inwardly on its own. A warm voice called out, "Come in, Caedmon, I should be glad of your company."

Before him was a small, lightly furnished room: one table and three old wooden chairs, none matching. A straw mattress lay directly on the floor newly made up with fresh linen. A fire of hickory wood burned on the hearth and while the majority chose to go up the chimney, some wafted through the room, smelling sweet.

A sense of heavy loss hung in the room, for when a child is gone, even a perfectly awful one, sadness lingers. Caedmon had been rehearsing an apology. He wanted to share the burden for the loss of Loman, to set forth some sense solidarity, but he could not find footing. Here before the hearth sat a strange purity of mourning. The lady's tears were unpolluted. She had no should-have-, might-have-, could-have-beens. Her mourning was free of self-doubt and inward angst. There was a purposefulness in her weeping that was beyond Caedmon's knowing.

Caedmon's mind flashed to his mother. His memory of her was dimming and his loss of her left raw and unprocessed. His home had been a whirl of confusion long before the killings. All interaction, both pleasant and unpleasant, was burdened with royal propriety and correctness of courtesy. No one knew his own mind, much less another's. Caedmon realized, looking at the lady before the fire, that while he could still picture his mother's face, and remember the touch of her kiss, he had not known her.

The lady of the house motioned for Caedmon to join her by the fire. He set down his staff and pulled up a chair and, as he sat beside her, her sorrow settled into his bones. With sorrow came knowledge—the loss of Loman was no one's fault but Loman's. The loss had nothing to do with not being loved.

"Do you spin?" she asked, her hand at the wheel, balls of wool in a basket by her feet.

"No, ma'am."

"Then you should learn. It unwinds the tears and lets them flow freely."

"So does a walk, ma'am."

The woman laughed a hearty ageless laugh that came up from her toes pouring out through her wide smile.

"I knew you would do me good, Caedmon."

"How do you know me? ... Mrs. ..."

"Call me Hilda."

"Mother Hilda, we have never spoken before this hour. How do you know me?"

"I know all who come to me."

"Do many come and refuse to stay?"

"Too many."

"Why, Mother Hilda? You are so beautiful and loving."

"To some my love is nettles and stings."

And with that she sighed and kept on spinning.

"Caedmon."

"Yes, Mother."

"Some come as Somebody and must learn that they are Nobody. Some come as Nobody and must learn they are Somebody."

"Yes, Mother ... I hardly know which I am."

"You brought with you an injury that needs tending. No cure, mind you, much of your wound will remain and you must adapt. It will bear useful fruit only in years to come."

Caedmon's head dropped. Big tears fell to the floor, pooling around his boots.

Chant-like Hilda soothed, "Rest. Weep. Rest. Weep. Rest. Weep. Repeat." The sweet hickory smoke pulsated around them both, deep and heavy.

Time passed, whether an hour or five Caedmon did not know. Mother Hilda spoke finally, "I must go out. My absence will only be matter of days."

Caedmon sighed, then looked into her bright face, "Do you want me to keep the cottage clean while you are away? I have heard there are certain chores ..." A half-attempted grin labored to appear on his lips.

Hilda patted his hand. "The assignments of another do not belong to you."

Caedmon no longer strained to smile.

"Must you leave? I have only arrived."

"It must be. Only one can stay in the cottage at a time and you are my chosen guest. But you are far from the only one who calls out for me."

With this she placed her hand on his head, assuring him that her cottage and quiet were enough with which to begin. She put on her cloak and disappeared into the dark forest.

Caedmon first took off his boots, and then every stitch of clothing. He sank into a warm tub in the kitchen. Barely awake he crawled out into the linen sheets and slept, waking only to weep, as unwept tears begged be let go, and sleeping once again.

Next morning he saw the tub had been drained and cleaned. And without the completion of a single chore, a loaf of fresh baked bread and a pitcher of milk appeared in the second cupboard. It was to appear again each sunrise and of this meal he never grew tired.

Each evening Caedmon would find a steaming tub inviting him for a soak and afterward he would tumble only partially dry into fresh linen. These ministrations worked so deeply on his soul that it did not matter how they happened but only that they did. By the fourth morning his grief abated, and as he ate his meal he found he was able to see outside himself again.

Looking about with fresh eyes, he spied a tall grandfather clock standing silent in the corner. But the silent timepiece did not hold his gaze for long. Caedmon spied what seemed a door behind. Sliding his hand behind the bulky clock, he found a latch waiting. It lifted eagerly and a door swung outward towards the garden. Expecting bright sunshine and open sky, rows of lamb's ears and mountain asters, instead he stepped out onto a wide alabaster floor. A stately room met him, lit uncannily from below—a lordly hall daunting even to a prince's son.

In addition to the footlights, a gallery of large paintings were individually illumined. Caedmon could not tell their number, as the works of art disappeared into the darkness as he walked past. Lighting depended on tread. The floor lit up tile by tile under the weight of his step. A pace before and a step behind glowed brightly but no more. Three tiles at a time was all that was offered. By the footlights, coupled with the glow of the paintings, one could see pillars that stretched from floor to an imagined ceiling somewhere high in the darkness.

Caedmon was sure a room of this size did not fit within the cottage. He wondered what trick of time and space might be at work to achieve such a wonder.

The first painting was of a blue summer sky. Fleecy clouds hung over green hills, streams darting down their sides. On the face of the hill wandered a flock of sheep attended by a shepherd dog and a little girl. Her bare feet dangled in the brook and the wind blew her hair back from her rosy face. Caedmon studied the picture. He drew closer and closer, feeling a pull of the wind on the hill. Mesmerized, he lifted a foot and found it was possible to step over the edge of the frame—the picture pulled and tugged as if desirous. Disoriented, Caedmon recoiled. Relieved to find he was still in the grand mysterious hall, his sense of security turned to caution. Perhaps, he thought, I should wait for a proper tour from the hostess. He would look at just one more painting, but with prudence.

Far down the high wall, a work of art caught his eye and less than a minute later he stood before it, absorbed. A glen under moonlight hovered lovely and lonely, set apart in the great hall. A tiny house stood distant in the background, its windows shuttered, its thatched roof criss-crossed in perfect evenness. In the foreground a young woman dressed in white gleamed under a well-lit night sky. Her hair flowed back just past her arching shoulders with head tilted up, eyes closed. Hers was the loveliest face and form that the prince had ever seen and it seemed that she was dancing for an audience of one —the moon. The painting was lit like the others but glowed with a light of its own.

So enraptured was Caedmon that he did not hear the door

behind the clock open and close. Nor did he hear the approaching figure. He was lifting his foot to enter the wide green moonlit glen when he felt a hand on his shoulder.

Startled, he jumped and whirled about. Mother Hilda stood with a piercing stare.

He stuttered out like a child caught, "You think I am here too soon ..."

Her nod was almost imperceptible.

"Oh, Mother, something so lovely after all my woe."

"You will come back to me with a new kind of sorrow."

"Oh, yes, Mother, I promise I will come back."

Hilda said nothing but sighed and brought forth his staff out from the folds of her cloak. She bent his head down to her lips, kissed him high on the forehead then whispered, "There is more to that staff than you know, but even what little you know will help you find your way."

Caedmon had hardly heard. He had already stepped through.

[7]

CAEDMON IN THE GLEN

THE TREETOPS of the surrounding wood parted for Caedmon as he stepped in through the frame. The great hall and Hilda closed behind him and he drifted downward. Magic between worlds held open until his foot ground into the forest floor. Caedmon did not look back or wonder about a return. The lady in the glen was his only thought.

Arriving at the edge of the clearing he saw a young woman near his age dressed all in white. She moved trancelike in a dance both well-practiced and spontaneous. Caedmon remained shrouded in the trees. There was an unseen boundary here between forest and glen, akin to the lawn at Hilda's house. The young woman's expressiveness out under the open sky was intensely intimate, belonging only to herself and heavenly watchers. Caedmon felt a wave of shame like one spying but he was a man immovable, as if chained to one of the great trees.

The watching prince's self-consciousness was replaced by wonder as her transparent spirit captivated him. He was given over, attuned to her every movement with the same depth as she was attuned to the music within. As she circled, her head tilted upward towards the heavens as one listening. Caedmon marveled at what unbearably beautiful music could produce the lilting measured movement.

She danced three rotations round the glen and then stopped a stone's toss away. Caedmon felt certain she had become aware of him but could not think of how he might confess his presence without startling her. The lady's arms fell to her sides and she broke into a long clear childlike laugh, musical as a stream over stones. Breathing heavily she threw herself on the grass, and lay gazing upward at the moon.

Face up she began to sing. Her soft soprano was sweet and lyrical, clear tones absent of all vibrato, untrained and aching—

> *Come nightfall, winds which cross the seas*
> *Blow east the rich perfume*
> *Vines waking to old memories*
> *Wrap arms around the moon*
> *When common sense attempts his shout*
> *A single bloom in single bar*
> *With single note does drown him out*
> *Backed by a choir of stars.*

These were all the lyrics Caedmon could grasp. More lines came, incomprehensible but no less stirring.

She remained for a long time out in the open, defenseless and unaware. For a while she sang, then fell to humming, at last settling into silence. Caedmon ventured no nearer. The fact that both of them existed in the same world, in such close proximity, was enough.

When Prince Caedmon at last broke from his reverie, it was daylight and the lady in the clearing had disappeared.

No TRACE of the dancer remained. Not a footprint lay before him on the meadow and overwhelming doubt raised its ugly head. Knowing these misgivings led to nowhere but madness, Caedmon busied himself with practical matters. He built a lean-to, foraged for berries and nuts, and devised schemes for a more permanent dwelling. By these measures Caedmon kept his wits, for he was determined to stay put to see if the lady reappeared. That night, she did.

The moon's glory waxed full when she rose and with her all Caedmon's doubts vanished. The lady shined in gold attire, shoes glimmering through the grass like fireflies. Orbiting the meadow in pirouettes she came. He scarce could take her in.

Before she began her second encircling, the clouds gathered curtaining the moon, the wind rose, and the trees moaned leaning before it. Prince Caedmon feared his beloved would leave, but she danced on despite the clouds that continued to congregate and the growlings of distant thunder. As the noise grew, again Caedmon agonized she would make her exit, but the young woman continued the dance. Then a sudden flash of blinding lightening shot through the clearing. When the ringing crash dissipated and Caedmon regained his vision, he saw—to his horror—the lady lay upon the ground. Out of the trees he bound to her, terrified of what he might find.

The young woman heard his approach and was on her feet in an instant but whether to fly or fight Caedmon could not tell.

"What do you want?" she demanded.

"I beg your pardon. I thought ... the lightning." Caedmon said, stuttering in great shock.

"There's nothing the matter." was her curt reply. And with that, she haughtily waved him off.

There was nothing to do but turn and walk back towards

the woods. But in a breath the lady reversed herself and he was recalled.

"Come back," she said "are you good?"

"Not so good as I should like to be." said Caedmon. He stood before her waiting, taking in her piercing blue stare. She motioned for him to follow.

Five steps behind her, he followed in her wake across the field, supposing she sought shelter in the cottage from the brewing storm. But around the bend, behind a small protruding grove, stood an arbor. It had corner pillars of planted oak, trained vines forming partial walls, and a roof matching precisely the thatch of the cottage. Though the wind blew through, the rain could make no entrance from above. A wicker bench of willow branches, worn but sturdy, sat in the corner and the lady motioned for Caedmon to sit. To sit while a woman stood scraped hard against all courtly education but Caedmon complied.

"Answer me this, then, good man," she began, like a professor giving an exam. "Describe for me the sun." Her brows furrowed in seriousness.

"What good is asking what you already know?" replied her befuddled pupil.

"But I don't know," she rejoined.

"Why, everybody knows."

"I'm not everybody and I have never seen the sun."

Caedmon stood bewildered.

"Is the sun as bright as she?" continued the young lady pointing at the full moon.

"Brighter. The sun is as bright as the lightning but shines steady like the moon, and rises and sets like the moon and shares her circular shape," replied Caedmon, taking his turn to play professor. "But it is so bright that you cannot gaze upon her."

"But I would look," his pupil inserted determinedly.

"But you couldn't."

"But I could."

"Couldn't."

"Could."

"Couldn't."

"Could!!!"

"Why don't you, then?"

"Because I can't."

Caedmon let out a heavy sigh and looked at the beautiful, earnest, stubborn face. He smiled and asked in one last effort, "Why can't you?"

"Because I can't wake. And I never shall wake until ..." And here the young lady stopped not because she did not want to tell, but because she did not know how.

Caedmon motioned for her to take the wicker bench.

"I think," said Caedmon, remembering etiquette, "that we need to properly introduce ourselves. Clearly by your manner and dress, you are a princess."

"And I think you must be a prince," said the princess from where she sat, enthroned on willows.

"And what make you think so?" asked Caedmon.

"Well, certainly not your dress," replied the girl. "By that you are part stable boy, part beggar."

Both broke out in wide smiles seen clearly in the moon's momentary fullness, for the storm had given pause, inhaling deeply for the next round.

"Then I must have excellent manners," said Caedmon. "Mother would have been proud."

"Would have been ...," pondered the princess in a quiet murmur.

"Now," interrupted Caedmon, "We must each decide how much to entrust to a complete stranger."

"I do not find you so strange."

"Believe me, my lady, our meeting is quite strange but that aside, I have seen enough even in my few years to teach me that a slow unfolding is better than a fast one."

"Nicknames." said the princess. "Let's share nicknames, and if we decide we are friends after swapping stories, we shall tell our true ones."

Caedmon saw her wisdom, surprising in one so obviously sheltered. Both of them needed company. Both were desperate for it. To hold back the intimacy of a name perhaps would help safeguard them both.

"Ok, my lady, call me Wes."

"Ok, dear prince, call me Gibby."

"Ah, after the moon."

"The moon?"

"Yes, waxing gibbous, when it is almost full. And waning gibbous as it shrinks towards crescent."

"I always thought Gibby to be boyish," she said mostly to herself. "Father's pet name makes more sense now."

"I shall go first," she declared bravely.

"As you wish," Wes replied.

[8]

GIBBY'S CONFESSION

THE RAIN FELL FORMING small pools around the arbor as it glided down off the smooth thatching of the roof. Gibby, though she had experienced the occasional admirer, was not practiced in speaking to suitors. She knew men came and spied her out, but men in the audience had never before come backstage to talk to the dancer. She, much like Caedmon, had never been given an opportunity to tell her story and floundered about on where to begin. Her start was high and formal.

"I am the only daughter of King Brychan and Queen Brevita of the province of Endelion." she began.

She halted, shoulders slumped. "Oh Wes ... I've already used real names. It's no use."

"Don't worry, I've never heard of them."

"Well, that's a relief ... I think. Really, never?"

"Please go on."

Confidence restored, Gibby continued, "My story begins before I was born, so I can tell some of it only as it was told to me."

Wes nodded.

"There was great jubilation in the land of Endelion for the first baby had been born to the queen and king. The wind and sun were out together and the palace flags frolicked against the blue sky." Gibby paused and looked towards Wes. "I was a beautiful, much hoped-for baby, Wes—bright eyes, cheerful disposition, the joy of the kingdom. An answer to my parents' fervent prayers."

Wes nodded. He felt he had heard this story somewhere before.

"Our palace is nestled on a hilltop just on the other side of that ridge." Here Gibby pointed to a group of three knolls just to the north. Each was completely covered with trees. Pines climbed up and over their rock faces and foreheads except the center one. The middle hill stood like an old man proud of his craggy clean-shaven skull.

"There is one disadvantage of living near a wood—fairies. Fairies always show up to greet a new baby, especially a princess. And among the fairies there is always a sour one—wicked, old, ugly, and ready to be offended, looking for pretext to turn a blessing into a curse."

Wes nodded again. He was quite sure he had heard a similar story before.

"At my christening five fairies were officially on the guest list and showed up with five gifts. Another one came to stand in the shadows with evil intent.

"You would think, Wes, that at a holy christening, I would be protected against all unkindness, but it was not so. My father says evil always transforms into good in time, but I think he may be oversimplifying. I am, after all, the one living the consequences."

"I believe you are getting ahead of the story," said Wes, but Gibby paid him no mind.

"Father always said, 'Look how it turned out for Sleeping

Beauty. Think of all the unworthy men who would have courted her. Did she not come awake exactly at the right moment when the right prince arrived?'"

Wes wondered what "right prince" meant exactly. Gibby plunged back into her tale.

"The five good fairies played by the rules. The one in the shadows looked for ways around them. Each of the five gave me gifts they counted best—beauty, song, charm, blah blah blah—and each stepped back into the crowd of devoted attendees. Then, into the surrounding splendor of the royal chapel stepped a toothless hag, bald but for the scrap of a widow's peak in front."

Here Gibby changed her voice to mimic an old toothless woman, "Please Your Grace, Mr. Archbishop, I'm very deaf. Would Your Grace mind repeating the princess's name?"

"And would you believe it, Wes, the hierarch of the church did not know what we both in our youth already understand. God forgive me for my anger and him for his foolishness but he gave the old crone my real name!" A frustrated tear ran down the princess's cheek. She wiped it away and continued with her toothless hag impersonation, "Little good shall any of her gifts do her. For I bestow upon her the gift of continuous sleeping, whether she will or not. Ha, ha! He, he! Hi, hi!" The court of course went into complete shock.

How did her parents not see this coming? thought Wes. This scenario is completely predictable.

Gibby pressed on. "To everyone's relief, out stepped a sixth good fairy. She had come in secret as a precaution against just such an event."

Wes admitted to himself he did not see *that* coming.

"If she sleeps all day," said good fairy number six, "She shall, at least, be awake all night."

"This well-intended kindness, of course, my prince of a

friend, was a great inconvenience to my parents. A baby does not care when she sleeps but my poor parents had to arrange a complicated schedule of staff. Extra nannies and housekeepers had to be hired. And my father the king, determined to be a hands-on parent, knew that sleepless nights before a long day at court are never good."

Putting again the grind of a dry axle into her voice, Gibby continued as the wicked fairy, screeching, "Out of order! I was interrupted before completing my evil laugh. Protocol has been broken!

"None could argue, not even the best lawyers present. So the old witch added to the damage already done. She spun a rune about poor choices, spoiled children, and the phases of the moon. It was clearly powerful but hard to discern—

> *Only child thy parents' delight*
> *Willful in the wakeful night*
> *Ne'er content you'll wax and wane*
> *Driving home your parents' pain*

"The court was scratching their heads and beginning to argue among themselves about the legalities of a double curse when a seventh and final good fairy stepped out of the crowd.

"Good fairy number seven added only anticlimactic ambiguity—a mysterious way the spell might be broken. She tried too hard to match the enigma of the curse. The antidote was worded so clumsily that the monthly 'What's to Become of the Princess Committee' chaired by the grand-duke is still arguing its meaning. Something about anonymity and a kiss, but the rhyme and rhythm were forced, making it jagged and unmemorable."

The princess again looked at Wes and asked rhetorically, "But what fool goes around kissing randomly, in secret, and, in my case, only at night? Dreadful not only for my reputation but devastating for all possible intimacy."

Wes had a rush of thoughts come to the surface but held his peace.

"The seventh fairy then added, as if to comfort the royals, 'Don't be afraid.' (Here Gibby used sarcastic air quotes.) 'The meaning will come with the thing itself.'

"After my christening, my parents endured many sleepless nights. The servants pitched in of course, and I am told I was a pretty happy infant. The second half of the spell, the one imbedded in the rune, did not come about till I was ten."

Gibby was now lost in thought and Wes stifled multiple urges to reach for her hand.

"Wes ..."

"Yes."

"I know it all sounds like some familiar fairy tale but that is because I have not told my part in it. I am no innocent victim. The weight of my own free will has come down harder than what was done to me."

"You were just a baby, Gibby," Wes said, his brow furrowing, "How can you be blamed?"

"Babies grow up and begin to make choices. If we are to be friends, Wes, I want to tell you the rest though you may not think well of me afterward."

Wes nodded.

"My parents spoiled me terribly. Not only was I their only child (my little brother was many years in the making), but I was 'special.' I was bewitched. The royal discipline that was my proper inheritance was not applied to me.

"As I grew, I became convinced that I was Somebody. I was the only daughter of a king and queen with a whole night staff at my beck and call. My parents were so proud of me, repeated everything I said, laughed and wondered and praised things that, in another child, would have struck them as unremarkable. My impertinent and rude actions were clever. My commonplace speech as marvelous as the finest poetry. I had excellent taste simply for choosing something shiny. Mother blamed the servants for making me vain but she would whisper flatteries to Father and I could hear every word. And I believed my specialness was fundamental, self-evident, and incontrovertible.

"By three years of age, no one dared tell me 'no.' Lighted candles were mine for the asking, a servant taking the greatest care so I would avoid the consequences of burned fingers and flaming frock. By seven, I was the center of my own universe. Instead of enjoying the things I had, I always wanted things I had not. My toys and dresses and pastimes were innumerable. Not only must I have everything, but I got tired of it almost as soon as I had it. I grew fond of animals but when I became angry I would beat them. And when they had lost their newness, I would neglect them. If they ran away, I became furious. If others cared for them, I grew envious. No pet in the palace would have survived if my tyranny did not sleep. And it did, each and every day. The bad witch had done the palace a great mercy in that aspect.

"The day of my tenth birthday I wandered depressed, blaming any but myself for my misery. I stumbled through the playroom door, past jeweled pocket watches and clockwork dolls, pet mice and rabbits, life-sized rocking horses imported from across several of the seven seas. I walked to the wide window and gazed out. Stepping out upon the broad balcony, I pointed at the sky and declared, 'I want the moon!'

"Staff hovered nearby, always afraid. One, brave or stupid, suggested a game of pretend. She fetched a thin platter of brilliantly polished silver, wide and perfectly round and held it out to me. An heirloom, it glimmered in the moonlight and reflected stars off its scalloped edges. I crossed the disheveled room and jerked it from her trembling fingers. Then I turned and flung the silver moon-shaped disc out into the night shrieking in rage. It was all the servants could do to keep me from flinging myself from the balcony after it. I sustained the ferocious violence for several hours before passing out.

"That night, the second part of the old hag's curse came down upon my head. I called it there and it still possesses me completely. I wanted to own the moon and now she owns me."

Wᴇs ᴋɴᴇw there was more to the tale told by the princess. But his ears were spent and his heart was worn by the forlorn look of absolute otherness that had come upon her. Inquisitiveness pulled up short and though queries stacked high and deep, explanations would wait for a time when sorrow was not so heavy. The prince ventured one last question that seemed a step outside the heartache.

"The song you dance to is beautiful, Gibby. Did you compose it?"

She shook her head.

"Your mother?"

She shrugged then whispered, "I think it was a fairy."

Wes knew it was now his turn to tell a tale but both of them were exhausted. He also was unpracticed and had so entered into Gibby's story, he had almost forgotten his own. Now, in his first attempt to tell his tale, more was left unsaid than was said. The princess bore the great weight of her own world and Wes did not think it right that she should bear his. He feared his wall of grief might break over her, dashing her upon sharp rocks.

In the end all the princess learned was that "Wes" was a prince of Morganstow and that he was traumatically orphaned. Gibby knew about orphans, but she had never heard of Morganstow. Wes found it impossible to speak of the hall of paintings and Mother Hilda. Gibby was familiar with unexplainable mystery, she lived under a fairy's curse after all, but one had to meet Mother Hilda to begin to understand. Hilda was the person on whom the prince's whole story hinged and Mother Hilda was no fairy.

Gibby listened dutifully and with all the keen interest her energy would allow. Then the two sat in silence until the princess grew unsettled. Sunrise was not long due.

She rose. "I am grateful for this night with you, Prince Wes. You have been good company." Wes grew alarmed. She was talking in past tense and he was sure this meeting was the first of many. A future was begging to unfold.

Gibby, seeing his distress, continued, "You carry sorrows brought upon you. I carry sorrows I brought upon myself. These are two very different burdens. There is only so much of life we can share."

"Both of us," Wes returned gravely, "are battling despair. It is a struggle best not done alone."

"But I must learn to repent and repenting *is* done alone. What have you to learn but to heal and survive?"

"I must learn to forgive and forgiveness and repentance are not as different as you might think."

She turned to go and Wes, desperate to secure a next time, blurted,"Do you live out here in the forest all alone? Do you ever visit your parents and the palace?"

"I must go, I will not have you carrying me to my bed in a dead sleep."

"How can I be of use to you? Will they ... can they help me at your father's house?"

"I do not know. I do not live there any longer. I never really did. Day staff is assigned to watch over my slumber out here in the cottage. It's an easy shift." She smiled, trying to make their parting less heavy. "I order the servants back to the palace each night."

"You have no company, no conversation?"

"People gawk. They come to see me dance, and hear the song, to see beauty. They want no more of me than that. Not really. To know more is to mourn the price."

Wes understood the comfort of solitude. "I am sorry I intruded."

"I am not," returned Gibby, smiling at him as she wiped another tear moving slowly down her cheek.

Then she hid her face in her hands, turned away, and walked towards the little house in the distance, the one Caedmon had noted in the painting. The perfect thatch shimmered, announcing the coming sun.

His desperate voice called out after her, "My true name, dearest princess, is Caedmon."

She turned, "Thank you, dear Caedmon. Your friendship was a gift."

The intimacy of his name, sacrificed for the momentary connection, seemed well spent.

"*Is*. Is a gift," Caedmon corrected.

Gibby looked at her friend pleadingly, "The fact that both of us communed under the same arbor for a single night is more than enough, and that you would entrust me with your name ..." Her countenance took on ten years, aged from the repetition of pain, "It is rare to find me as I am now, Caedmon. Go home."

The prince ventured to follow her at a little distance, but she waved him off. And he, a true gentleman, obeyed.

"Tonight was a thing of beauty," the princess called out but did not turn again, "and beauty is never to be regretted." She quickened her pace towards home.

The night was gone and Caedmon saw her no more again as she was that night, dancing under the moon.

[10]

CUTHBERT'S REPLACEMENT

Not more than twelve miles away, at the highest point of the kingdom of Endelion, the sun rose on the palace of King Brychan and Queen Brevita. They were just awakening as their daughter began slumbering like one dead in the adjacent valley.

Caedmon headed over the ridge following well-worn trails used by palace staff assigned to the princess. Up he climbed, down he lumbered, then up once more towards the distant palace. He had only a few hours to form his thoughts and sketch a plan of action. "Knowledge is power, my son," he heard his father's voice from more tender times. The advice had rolled off like so many other stodgy truisms of his youth, but now it seemed the only sensible course to follow. But how? He smiled, almost giggling, at the thought of a "What's to Become of the Princess Committee." He imagined slipping in to take minutes, incognito, sporting a fake beard and mustache among a group of old curmudgeons. But in his heart, Caedmon was sober. In this house, like his own, "committee" was just

149

another word for a smoke screen behind which royals hid insoluble sorrows.

The palace was grand. Its great front double doors beckoned. Caedmon was consoled by the lack of walls and that no gate barred the way. In Endelion's short history, the mountains around the kingdom had so far provided defense enough. Weathercocks spun in the wind and the sun shone on the flags whipping westward. On three sides lay woods so wide and dense that no royalty had yet explored the territory thoroughly. Main roads cut great swaths north, south, and west, but no more than footpaths claimed secondary inroads among the thick trees. The king and his courtiers often hunted, which kept the wild creatures at bay. Close in, all was trim and manicured, free from beasts and brush a hundred yards round, the work of three full-time gardeners.

With the confidence belonging to a prince, Caedmon approached the front doors, staff in hand. He was not sure who would answer and what he would say but he determined to make inquiries. He sidetracked but once upon noticing a pond of gold and silver fish to the west of the main walk. Caedmon had heard of man-made ponds and imported fish but he had never seen one himself. His delight in the fish was short-lived for his own reflection came back as a shock. Two years in the stables and weeks in the wild had transformed him. Rugged was too generous a word. How had he dared approach the feminine beauty he had conversed with the night before? "Well, Father," he murmured, "some knowledge is not empowering. I stand beholden to my ignorance."

Ignorant no longer, Caedmon scurried from the glorious front lawn and went in search of a more humble entrance. His nose led him to the kitchen door. Here he approached and knocked with a very clear plan—asking for a bit of bread. The good-natured cook refused his request and instead brought him in and filled his belly with a most excellent breakfast.

Prince Caedmon had never been served in a palace kitchen before. He knew something of what it meant to dine in the rooms above. He wondered if a version of his old life carried on overhead and for a moment his heart tightened in his chest. But here below, the rustic surroundings washed over him as a wave of immense relief. Intrigue, destitution, and prolonged anonymity had brought him low and in that moment he was glad to have slunk away from the palace's high entrance. He relished the hash and eggs on the tin plate in front of him. He savored, shoveling it in on day-old bread. Endelion was treating him well.

As Caedmon ate, pondering if perhaps observing royalty by serving royalty might help untangle his soul and mind, other servants came through—a gardener, a blacksmith, and the young prince's nanny. The men grabbed a bite and passed through in a rush but Nanny paused to query the cook, "So who's this s-strapping youth?" The cook opened her mouth to answer, but before she could Caedmon inserted himself. He rose with a bow, "Pleased to meet you, ma'am, I'm the new kitchen help."

"Replacing that numskull Cuthbert?"

"Definitely," answered Caedmon with a tone of one self-assured.

"Good," said the nanny emphatically but with a mild stutter, "mind your fingers with the p-paring knife. Its what did him in—that, and not w-washing."

"I will mind my fingers then," replied Caedmon.

Nanny and Cook both looked at each other and a knowing smile passed between them. Caedmon noticed and grew nervous.

"I hope I did not offend," he began, "Give me something to chop or dice or wash and I will prove my value."

At this Nanny and Cook not only looked at each other but burst into hysterics.

"Not again!" giggled Cook.

"Royalty sneaking into the k-k-kitchen," stuttered Nanny.

"Knows how to chop," wheezed Cook.

"He'll p-p-prove his value," hiccuped Nanny.

"Lost Prince Sous Chef," screamed Cook.

Both stood there dripping tears, trying to catch their breaths, patting each other on the back in gratitude for the mutual entertainment. With each exchange Caedmon's jaw dropped further, only adding to their merriment.

Finally Nanny had to scurry off to nursery duty. The young prince did not sleep all day like his older sister. She chortled all the way back up stairs trying to pull herself together to face her charge.

Caedmon was left staring at Cook.

"Don't worry," Cook said assuringly. "You have a job as long as you like or until you lose your fingertips like Cuthbert. Slow but sweet, he was, God bless him. Mind, you'll make small wages, very little past the food I give you."

"Thank you," breathed Caedmon, his face set and somber. "What do I call you, ma'am?"

"Ma'am, indeed." said Cook giggling once again. "Just call me Cook. We are what we do in the servant's quarters. When we find out what you do well, you'll have a name too. For now, what do you go by?"

"Wes."

"I bet that's not what they called you when you dined upstairs."

Wes leaned in and almost whispered, "How did you know

my rank, dressed as I am, smelling as I do? And besides, there will be no more dining upstairs for me."

"Oh, a royal with a sad backstory. That at least will be different than the last half dozen."

"Half dozen?" queried Wes, understanding but not wanting to.

"Half dozen that have seen her, thought they wanted her, swore they'd do anything to have her. And then left the way they came. Some it took a month, some a year. But they all leave when they see the impossibility of it ..." she trailed off.

Wes leaned forward hoping for more.

"Look, son, I like you. I'll most likely grow attached and then you'll leave just when you raise my hopes and win my heart. But the practical fact is we have meal prep for a brunch, a ladies' high tea, and dinner for more than forty in the king's hunting party. Plus, did I mention, it's the chief steward's name day and I promised to bake a cake."

Cook sighed.

Wes sighed.

"But ..." Cook continued, "if you are able to—how did you put it—'prove your value,' I'll have the energy to tell you the great mysterious story of our princess, the parts I know anyways."

"Thank you," breathed Wes, barely above a whisper.

"I did it for all the others, why not you," quipped Cook.

Never, even as a stablehand, did a young man work so efficiently and tirelessly as Wes did that day for Cook. That night, she kept her part of the bargain. For though exhausted herself, Cook loved to spin a story.

[11]

A LITTLE HOCUS POCUS

Wes sat in silence at the end of the long wooden kitchen table. Cook took a stool nearby and began—

"Living near a wood is lovely if you can put up with a fairy infestation and fairies are at the root of all of Gibby's woes. Most have gone into hiding but back when Gibby was born, several fairies lived quite openly within a few miles of the palace, regular addresses and their own zip code. Unfortunately for babies, royal babies in particular, they are a great fascination to fairies, for fairies can't have infants of their own.

"One fairy of particular talent broke fellowship with the rest. She was the oldest, and at one time, the wisest of the lot. But she could not stand the constant debate and discussion of how the community should be run. Efficiency was her high standard and if the others would but follow her benevolent lead, all would be done decently in good order. The politics and infighting that ended with her expulsion are past my understanding but in the end, without fairy fellowship, she lost her fairy beauty and charm. None of the villagers could tell her from an old crone and the fairies themselves hardly recognized her, who was once their sister. She withdrew to live alone in the darkest part of the forest, emerging only to trick people into offending her so she could take vengeance upon them. Nasty game.

"When royal babies are born in Endelion, kings and queens can't have a christening without the blasted fairies showing up. The majority come bearing remarkable gifts but it seems to me it's the common folk who need the leg up. I'd like to see what the royals could do on their own merits."

Cook turned to her listener, "No offense, Wes—you didn't have fairies at your christening, did you?"

Wes shook his head.

"Well, in my opinion, the value fairies bring does not outweigh their risk. It only takes one foul fairy to ruin a christening, one to cause a lifetime of damage. Of course the old hag showed up at Gibby's, there to do exactly as she liked and make excuses for it."

Cook turned again to her attentive audience, "It's the excuses, Wes, what turns my stomach. Do evil and be proud of it, I say. Don't put on airs and pretend. A little integrity ..." Cook sighed and continued.

"As best the doorkeeper could count, five fairies showed up. He, of course, did not count a wobbly old woman with a widow's peak and cane among the security risks. The obvious five came forward and presented charming grace-filled gifts, pleasant enough (though again, mind you, I think Gibby would have developed beautifully without the extra help). After they finished laying it on, old snaggletooth hobbled out into the middle of the chapel floor, eager to do harm. Teetering on the edge of senility she spouted—

> *Hocus pocus on me focus*
> *Sleeping beauty put to shame*
> *Never will you wake again*

"Those weren't, Wes, her exact words, but I get tired of telling it the same way to each prince. You don't mind a few creative liberties do you?"

Wes shrugged.

"Well that was the gist of the curse and of course the old warthog had to cackle afterward, 'Ha, ha! He, he! Hi, hi!'

"Here her cackle was interrupted. Interrupting is most always rude but when it comes to magic, butting in is down-right perilous. It seemed a small thing to cut off the wicked woman in her afterglow but on this interruption pivoted Gibby's future.

"A fresh-faced rookie of a good fairy did not let the old bat finish. In barely audible timid sweetness, she stepped forward in an out-of-turn attempt to counter the curse—

> *Hocus pocus on me focus*
> *Daytime sleeping is your fate*
> *But through the night be wide awake*

"This was a decent first spell, cast by a sixth good fairy. She came in with the five, held in reserve as a surprise tactic. The young trainee knew she was backup but hoped to just observe. Now she found herself in the thick of a battle just begun.

"The wicked fairy, well-versed in opportunistic offense, screeched, 'She spoke before I was done! Foul! Encroachment against the rules of decency and good order! I had only got to "Hi, hi!'

"No one could argue. She had not indeed rotated through all the vowels, an old little-known rule but one steeped in tradition. So the hag drew a deep breath and wove a second spell (knowing full well second-round runes do not pack near the punch)—

> *Hocus pocus spoke too soon*
> *She'll wax and wane with each new moon*
> *Ha, ha! He, he! Hi, hi! Ho, ho! Hu, hu!*

"The witch gave a florid triumphant bow and cast about for a grand exit.

"But the battle was not over. A seventh fairy, hidden in the crowd, even more timid than the sixth, said in a tiny whisper—

"'*Hocus pocus* ... oh fudge, I can't make a rhyme to save my s-soul. Can I begin again?'

"The crowd nodded politely as one, heads turning together if watching badminton. Fairy Seven seemed so weak in the ways of magic and her voice instilled no hope in the onlookers, but at least it was a first-round spell and that was a small encouragement.

"'Until ... ' the seventh fairy stuttered 'Until ... a p-prince comes who shall k-kiss her without knowing it.'"

Here Wes leaned in sharp, stopping Cook. "Say that again."

"Say what again?"

"The seventh fairy's spell."

"No one really knows precisely what she said. She was always whispering, that plus her speech impediment ..."

"It matters very much to me. It is the only part that is new," begged Wes.

"New?"

"Gibby told me."

"You've talked with our princess?"

"Why of course. Did not the others? Am I not only one of many?"

Cook gave a low whistle, "The others watched her dance, admired her beauty, desired to free her from the spell and marry her at once. But none had the spine to talk to her. She's not particularly approachable with all the dancing, singing, waving at the moon. And then she disappears into that little hut of hers before dawn with the precision of a cuckoo clock."

Cook added with a huff, "I feel like an idiot spinning my yarn to a warmed over audience. Why did you let me go on and on?"

"It is best to listen and not interrupt."

"True, but is also deceptive to act as if you know nothing when you know plenty."

"It is good to get another perspective on matters of import."

Cook had no answer except to bring her tongue to a grinding halt.

She yawned and stretched, "It's late, Prince Wes. I have more to say but I will not say it unless you give two promises."

Wes was tired. Wes promised.

Cook laid out her conditions, "One: you will stop my storytelling in its tracks if my telling is a repetition. Two: you will arise before dawn tomorrow ready to work. Agree to both else you will not earn more from my wagging tongue."

Wes was glad for simple, straightforward, rhyme-free conditions.

12

MORE THAN HE WANTED TO KNOW

Wᴇs's second day in the kitchen proved much more exhausting than the first. A bumper crop of muscadine grapes had come in to be canned. Jelly was a staple in the diet of the queen and waste was unthinkable. Wes wondered at the process, having never thought before of the labor behind the jars of sweetness magically appearing on a king's table. He sweated uncomplaining over the boiling pots. However, what with sweeping up shattered jars, sorting out sour grapes, and having regular meals to prepare as well, both he and Cook were too tired to even say goodnight, much less converse further about the princess's bewitchment.

Cook let him sleep well past sunrise the third day of his employment. When he did reach the kitchen he was relieved to find that besides baking fresh bread, the palace required nothing of the kitchen staff that day. The royals had deemed it "leftovers day" and for this sensible prudence Wes was thankful. Stable work for six horses did not compare to the constant activity demanded in a kitchen that fed more than one hundred and twenty souls.

That evening Wes answered an invitation to Cook's small room. Though less eager than two nights before, he wanted to see the story through. As he entered, Nanny was rising to go. Something in their combined company made him miss Mother Hilda though he could not pinpoint why. His thoughts on the matter were broken up by a gentle command to sit.

Fruit juice left from the canning adventure and the last of a loaf of fresh bread was set between them. Cook put her feet up on an apple crate and folded her hands across what once was her waist. "Where were we, kitchen boy?" she asked with a wink. "You have more than earned the rest of my tale."

How could Wes forget? She had left off with "... and a prince comes who shall kiss her without knowing it." A stone ricocheted from the pit of his stomach, scraping raw the lower recesses of his heart. "I think," he told Cook, "The next part might be what came from all the spells and magic."

Cook nodded, "You remember our agreement though: no letting me go on and on thinking myself clever about facts you already know."

"Yes, ma'am."

"Promise."

"Gibby said little more. The sun was rising."

Cook glowered at him and then her face softened. Growing serious once more, she dove again in.

"After the seventh fairy's stuttering excuse for a spell, the crowd who had assembled for the christening broke up, feeling rather miserable. Queen Brevita prepared for her future of sleepless nights. A new nanny was hired because the old one found the night shift unbearable. King Brychan made good his determination to fulfill his fatherly role and adjusted his schedule to begin late morning, volunteering to aid in the first watch of the night.

"Eventually the household settled into a regular system,

taking shifts. The early days were joyful. The wicked spell had not reached the baby's heart. Like clockwork, she dropped asleep at the first hint of dawn in the east. And there was no awakening her before sunset. No, the forest could burn down about her ears, her cradle lifted up by a great cataract, the palace collapse in a mighty earthquake and the princess would slumber on. The happiness continued for two years and it seemed the mystery of the old hag's second stab had been side-stepped. But some curses need human cooperation. Parents and palace servants stumbled in their responsibilities. We treated the young human like she were a god, doting on her and fawning for her favor, and the results were monstrous."

Here Cook paused. She put her face in her hands and began to weep silently, shoulders shaking. Wes sat helpless.

Cook wiped her face on her apron, adding another stain to a long history of stains. "I am betraying my mistress to tell you more. I should have never begun ..."

Wes placed a hand on hers. She laced her fingers through his. "Do not worry, Mother Cook," he whispered, "Gibby told me. I know of her terrible behavior and what ensued. You have not betrayed. I love your mistress too."

"She told you the hard unflattering parts?"

"As if I were her confessor."

"You *are* the first ..." but Cook broke off. Her story continued now with the gravity of a great unburdening.

"As you know, from Gibby's tenth birthday, the new moon lorded over us all. We began then to endure much more than sleepless nights.

"When the moon was at the full, my mistress was in glorious spirits and as beautiful as it was possible for a child of her age to be. But as the moon dwindled, she faded, becoming sickly, like a waif lying the arms of a homeless mother. When the moon waned past third quarter she became as one dead—

not speaking, not eating, with barely a breath. I've heard told that when the moon is new and disappears she becomes something else altogether … but who am I to tell that part? I've never seen it with my own eyes."

Cook faded off. Then began again.

"For the seven years since she turned ten, every month she skirts death. As soon as the moon waxes she improves. By the first quarter she begins to move her lips and those who stand by her bed give nourishment. By the time the moon passes into waxing gibbous she sings again, and when the moon is full, she dances in earnest, savoring full strength for the few days she is able. In solitary moonlight she is her happiest.

"Her father and mother arranged the palace staff to meet her needs. All royal business bent to the state of the princess. The moon bound the kingdom to the lunar calendar. But the princess grew to dislike being seen, still more being touched.

"A little cottage was built, and Gibby wanted nothing more. A space on the edge of a great open glade was chosen, near the palace but tucked out of sight. The location provides a vista through the trees where the princess can always see the moon as it passes through the heavens whether waning or waxing. Here she enjoys what little freedom her bewitchment allows."

Cook sighed and wiped her brow, all at once overcome by fatigue.

"Our princess's beauty has attracted more than one would-be suitor. But in reality no king in his right mind wants her for a daughter-in-law. Young men come full of themselves with something to prove. They go away defeated when they see the tragic hopelessness."

Cook stopped here having run out of steam. She closed her eyes and reached for the final slice of bread, humming an old tune. Wes had listened so well she had forgotten he was present. Before the crust had reached her mouth she began to sing—

> *Would-be lover you aim too high*
> *My master will not let me go*
> *I may see you for but one night*
> *Please leave before I bring you woe*
>
> *Would-be lover run on home*
> *My master will not let me go*
> *Find comfort in the stable maid*
> *No shame is found in loving low.*

Wes let himself out while Cook slaughtered the third verse, lyrics long forgotten. As he made his way through the darkness to his bed, he remembered the sweet simplicity of Kassia walking with him to the final gate.

13

THE NIGHT BEFORE THE NEW MOON

THE NEXT MORNING Cook found a note.

Dear Cook,

I am grieved to leave you. It was blessed time working elbow to elbow with you. But as you astutely surmised, I am a prince. I would grow restless as kitchen help even under your excellent tutelage.

I know you and Nanny were hoping I was the one to free Gibby. Sadly, I am not.

I will treasure the time with you always,

Prince Caedmon of the kingdom of Morganstow (what's left of it)

Bewildered, Cook showed the note to Nanny before tucking it into her apron pocket. Nanny knew well the talkative good intentions of her childhood friend. Tamping down a rising tone of accusation, Nanny inquired, "What all did you t-tell him?"

"More than any of the others, my dear. He earned it,"

replied Cook, quashing a rising defensiveness. Nanny raised a brow and Cook continued, "By earned I don't just mean the work for me—he was only so-so as a sous chef. But his work with *her*. All the other idiot princelings sat and drooled and spoke of her beauty. Wes, I mean Caedmon, is the first who entered her pain ... no, that sounds stupid. How should I put it? He saw *who* she was under the pretty face."

Cook heaved an unsatisfied sigh, wishing for better words. Nanny held her peace.

"Why should he not be entrusted with more?" Cook queried, her tone rising, arms crossed over her sagging breasts. The next second she softened, admitting, "Talking to him was strangely relieving ... unburdening myself of the whole thing. Anyhow, he knew most of the tale already ... direct from the little mare's mouth."

Nanny looked down and took a deep breath, and then up into the searching eyes of a friend she knew always valued truth, "And n-now he knows *t-too* much."

There was a long pause, too long, considering Cook's life experience and quick intelligence. She gasped, jerking her hand to her mouth. "What I have I done ... and he was so ... so perfect." The tears were coming fast, and with a heart-rending sob she blurted "He was the best of the lot so far!"

Nanny sat beside her arms-round, rocking Cook as she cried.

Before he set out, staff in hand, Caedmon also wrote a note to his long-dead father, a note impossible to send but it felt good to write anyhow.

Dear Father,

Which of our forefathers said, "Do not tell your grief to a lesser man; tell it to your saddle-bow and ride forth singing?" I never understood the quote's wisdom before now. I have neither saddle nor bow but I have found pen and paper and you are not a lesser man.

Why do women think that talking helps? While listening wins hearts, and a woman's heart is a great treasure, the facts gained are unbearably burdensome. Is this why men grow forgetful? I have gained more knowledge through ladies of late than I can process in ten years. Along the way, I have lost my heart.

You said to me in my studies that knowledge is power, the power of kings. But too much knowledge has made me powerless. How can I be the prince who kisses "without knowing" when I know so much? I wish you walked beside me now to help me understand.

Your firstborn,

Caedmon

Caedmon tossed the note into the hearth and stepped out of the servant's quarters. Leaning hard against the exterior wall he stifled an ugly cry, then set out. None heard him leave, none saw him go except the flame that flickered up devouring his handwriting.

Prince Caedmon from the kingdom of Morganstow headed back over the hills to the residence of the princess of the kingdom of Endelion. He did not know her name but she knew his. She did not know who he was nor where he came from but he knew her whole history. He traveled full speed intending to bid both his first and final goodbye.

The distance between the cottage and palace seemed to him to have doubled. More than once he lost his way in the wood which felt to have tripled in its thickness of thorny vine and quadrupled the number of fallen oaks across once-clear paths. The half-day trip cost him two.

The first night he crawled into a hollow yew tree, held his knees, and wept. Clouds covered the moon and stars. In the total darkness he noticed for the first time that his staff, the gift from Mother Hilda, glowed at his touch. If he put it down in the dark it disappeared. If he gripped it tight it sputtered and went out. But if he held it loose in his palm and placed his forefinger on an almond-shaped knot two-thirds of the way up from the slender end point, it glowed. It was a strange comfort and was all that kept him from complete despair. Something about its color reminded him of the wise woman's eyes when she was her most stern.

Gibby's cottage finally came into view on the second night, the journey made possible and almost pleasant by the light of the staff. When last he had seen the cottage, he had been shooed away, but now under a moonless sky the staff led him one step at time across the wide field. With open hand he knocked upon the door. No answer. With closed fist he knocked again. Still nothing. With the top of his glowing staff he rapped seven times, even-spaced. The door cracked open and a bulging eye pressed through staring up and down at its visitor. Wide open it swung and Caedmon was pulled inside. The door slammed shut in his wake.

A GIRL in tatters crouched on a high stool before him. A single candle was lit in the corner. Her chin sunk on her chest and she stared down at her own gnarled toes. Her face was the color of pale earth, with a pinched nose, and a mere slit in her face for a mouth.

Compassion and horror filled Caedmon. He put out a hand to touch her but she scampered away and leapt onto a nearby table.

"Who are you?" he asked.

"Who are you?" she returned sounding like an echo.

"I am Wes."

"No you're not. You're Caedmon!" She then repeated the information to herself in a sing-song manner.

"No you're not. You're Caedmon. Prince Caedmon. You're Caedmon."

The girl remained crouched, hopping like a frog back onto the stool that tottered on three of its four legs beside her visitor. She reached out and patted him on the head as if he were her pet.

"You are Caedmon and I am B," she said, looking everywhere but at him. Then with the air of an elementary teacher she informed her reluctant guest, "When you are bad, they take a letter away. I am now just B." She pulled at her own hair, stringy and yellow, and rocked repeating, "Just B, just B, just B …"

"Are you quite alone, B?" asked Caedmon glancing about the room.

"Only at night. They always come back during the day for B," she answered. Then turning a lipless smile his way, she cooed, batting lash-less lids, "But you are here now. It's nice to have a visitor at night."

Over her face spread such an odious, self-satisfied expression, that Caedmon felt ashamed for her even as his stomach churned. The girl began to pat her own cheeks, to hug her own shoulders, and examine her own finger-ends, all the while nodding her head with deep satisfaction.

"You love me, Caedmon, I know. Dedicated to my health and happiness. You are not much as yet but will become the prince I deserve."

All was said without so much as a glance in Caedmon's direction. He was present, but not. Rocking, her arms hugged her own body ever tighter. "Deserve, dear B, deserve. He's the prince you deserve."

Caedmon shuddered at the thought of ever being caught in such arms. He took a step back towards the door. "I came to visit someone else. And though I wish you happiness, I must go."

The candle went out on its own. Something in Caedmon knew the door was poised to lock on its own as well. Once locked in, he knew not even the light of his staff could guide him through the bottomless pit of need. There was a scuttling in the dark first in one corner and then the opposite.

The staff flickered as he hesitated but Caedmon's feet saved him. Used to being on the move, they walked him backwards towards the door on their own. His eyes sought the creature in the dark but found her not. Behind his back he reached and popped the latch. At the sound of the click she sprang, arms sprawled, teeth bared. A single step more and he was out on the moonless step. The door slammed and her airborne body thudded against it.

Light was flickering in the east, a servant was making her way up the hill. Caedmon darted around the cottage to escape notice and leaned against a window pane breathing hard. Over his heaving sobs came a clear, untrained, vibrato-free soprano scraping its way through a crack in the glass—

Silver platter
Silver spoon
Gimme gimme
Mine's the moon

Darling prince
You leave so soon
Promise me ...

Silence fell as the sun rose. Grief and shame tried to drive Caedmon into the forest but he had no spirit left to move his feet. He made it as far as the cottage woodpile and collapsed behind it. The weather was warm. It was a good place to hide a broken prince for the servants needed no kindling.

The sun was high in the sky when kisses woke Caedmon. Wet kisses. Tongue kisses. He blinked awake to find himself loved by a shepherd dog.

[14]

FAIRIES IN THE FOREST

CAEDMON KNEW ENOUGH about dogs to know when he was being shepherded. He submitted himself like a lamb, indifferent to where he was being taken. In this low hour, loss and life rubbed shoulders.

Bleary-eyed, he followed his four-legged guide back into and through the forest looking only down. One foot flopped in front of the other upon a fading path. So transfixed was he upon his own trudging feet that the dog took to nudging, pressing guidance on first one side then the other. The hapless man did not see the spider webs stretch across the way or care about the branches reaching and scratching.

Possessing all of Caedmon's mind was the image of a lipless, lashless face. He saw the girl, golden and glorious, devoured by the shrunken and self-obsessed. Then came floating before him two faces set on a single ivory neck swiveling back and forth, back and forth, in silent insistent negativity. Cook's words echoed, "I've heard told that when the moon is new she becomes something else altogether." Cook's phrases folded into the same sing-song rhythm imbedded in his

171

brain by B the night before: "No you're not, you're Caedmon, Caedmon, Caedmon." B's mocking tone modulated and transformed into, "I heard told she's something else, something else, something else ..." Finally, B's and Cook's voices merged into one fiendish chorus sung by the oscillating head of Gibby-B, "No you're not you're something else, you're Caedmon, Caedmon. No you're not you're something else ..." Caedmon came to a dead stop upon the path. His hands pressed hard on his ears. His breathing accelerated. The staff of Hilda dropped clattering to the forest floor. Swallowed up in a great terror of nothingness, the young prince saw neither the path nor his feet upon it.

In the next instant, shock and sharpness brought Caedmon back. There was neither blood nor bruise, but stabbing pain and sharp bark brought the young man back to himself, driving the sing-song voice of despair out and away over the silent watchful trees. The dog, duty bound, having stooped to ferocious bark and violent bite, now wildly wagged his tail. Caedmon shook his head clear and reclaimed both staff and wits.

With a composed mind came questions: Had Cook seen what he had? Doubtful. And if Cook had, her loving nature would have dissuaded, not encouraged. How long had the dog been guiding him? Hours? Days? Whose dog was he?

As Caedmon took in his surroundings, the dog gave up his herding. The man had clearly begun to faithfully follow. Webs and branches were again knocked aside as the human's head tilted up instead of staring down.

For his part, Caedmon could tell by the wag of the tail that the two of them were nearing the hound's intended goal. The good character of his guide lightened his steps in anticipation.

Ahead towards evening, seven trees stood: an alder, a beech, a birch, a chestnut, a hickory, an oak, and a yew. Never had Caedmon seen seven species grouped this way, but they were as real as himself and his canine guide, roots sunk deep in the loamy soil. The seven trunks grew in a perfect ring, equal distance apart, equal in circumference, equal in height. Nature did not produce such symmetry.

Lifting high his chin, Caedmon saw great branches above the circle of trunks woven together forming a domed roof. Turf and moss filled in as shingles. Supporting, intertwining sprigs hugged the stone chimney puffing in the southeast corner. The rising rings of smoke, like the sound of a dinner bell, caused Caedmon's hunger to leap upon him. Cautiously he set out to walk full circle around the structure. But his canine guide lost patience, licked his hand, and pulled the man by the tattered shirtsleeve towards the entrance. Between yew and alder hung a yellow door, snug within the mortared wall of river stone fitted between the trees. Caedmon grasped his staff, wondering what manner of knock might be best, but the great dog leapt against the doorway and inward it swung wide open on its rustic hinges. Caedmon stood dumbfounded in the entry, the arches of his feet wobbling on the threshold.

In a large, spacious, circular room set seven rocking chairs, each a different shade of green. Five were occupied. Behind each chair, several yards back, was a door sunk into the bark of a hollowed-out tree, seven portals into and out of the great vaulted common area. Five heads bobbed up from ten busied hands and cried, "Excellent job, Prince! Good boy!!" Five women rose and rushed, pouring affection upon one well–pleased dog. In a short space the dutiful hound, satiated by the shower of petting and praise, drew back and threw himself down on the hearth rug. All maternal attention then turned towards the puzzled guest.

"Prince has brought in a prince," said one.

"Let him sit," said another, rising to pull their visitor in and shut the yellow door against the coming night.

"Feed him," said a third, much to Caedmon's delight.

"Sorry for the muddle," interjected the fourth, "We named our dog Prince. It's so nice to call and have one come."

The fifth lady of the house served stew from the pot near the fire and added a slice of cold cheese on the side of an earthenware plate. She placed it on the large stump in the middle of the room, the remnant of a massive ash tree. The ash, once towering over the circle of seven, now served as table, round and ground down. Glancing around, Caedmon noted that besides the rockers, the truncated ash was the only furniture in the wide spacious room.

Fairy the Fifth motioned for Caedmon to occupy an empty chair and to take up and eat. "Don't worry," she said, "We've eaten and the seat's not taken. Two of us choose to live and work elsewhere."

Caedmon sat. Caedmon ate. And by his fifth bite he knew, just as he knew his own name (Caedmon, not Wes), that this was the very flight of fairies present at Gibby's christening.

As both princes ate, human and hound, each fairy busied herself with her handiwork. It did not take long for Caedmon to finish and his plate was filled again and again. Quietness was observed, as was the case during all meals in Fairy Bower, and the ladies busied their hands. Three knitted and two sat and spun great wads of yellow wool. Replenished, Caedmon's heart slowed, beating in time with the whirling spindles. Leaning his head backward in the rocker he traced the maze of lattice work in the roof of the ringed arbor. The sap hummed as it ran up and down the branches, warming and resonating within each interlocking limb—

> *Alder, Hickory, Chestnut, Yew*
> *All my woes are nothing new*
> *Oak and Birch and stately Beech*
> *All your wisdom's past my reach*

The heart of the trees bent together down as if desiring to scoop Caedmon up among their stately boughs and rock him to sleep like a babe. All he had seen, felt, and endured came cascading—small connections, hidden meanings, hints of what he was to learn, promises of wisdom. Woven through in the branches above lay threads of understanding to come in due time. But for now all lay beyond the mind of the exhausted prince. The tender voices of the trees rested in wordless depths. Caedmon's awareness of the mystical went no further than an inkling that he sat in Nanny's chair and that the empty wicker seat across the room belonged to Cook.

The prince looked down from the reverie of the roof into the center of the circular room. The ash table sat, sanded smooth and subservient. Its deep roots boasted of soaring branches that once hung immense, fearsome to behold. How far the mighty must have fallen and how great the fall of her! Were the roots dying in the ground or growing stronger as they nestled in the arms of mother earth? Sorrow and dread tiptoed hand-in-hand.

Fairy the Second watched the Caedmon's wandering eyes, dropping her hands from her spindle. In silence, she glided across the room ever closer until she came almost nose to nose with their guest. Her eyes stared into his. "Do not borrow sorrow," she commanded, just under a whisper.

Then, taking Caedmon's hand in hers, she placed in his palm a wad of yarn, an invitation to join. Fairy the Second returned to her spindle and Caedmon set his hands to usefulness.

NOT LONG AFTER Caedmon had wound his third ball of yellow twine, Fairy the First broke the silence, "You have seen and spoken to Princess Bridget twice now, Caedmon. The first time you were filled with love for her. What of the second?" Her knitting needles clicked together with sudden fierceness.

Caedmon felt taken aback by the sudden encroachment. The deepest matters of his heart were were now laid upon the table. A stinging shame caused him to balk. Why should Gibby's true name have been announced so unceremoniously?! He looked about from face to face and knew they already knew, but still, each expected full disclosure. Caedmon answered in jest, "Fairies *do* dive in."

No one laughed.

Caedmon's mind raced. He bore indelible marks from a childhood ravaged by palace politics and royal propriety. And though he detested duplicity, he was comfortable with secrecy cloaked as discretion. It was familiar. The fairies' pointed communication caused him to shrink. The ten eyes that looked upon him were indispensable to his survival, each appeared to know and even understand, but their kindness still felt invasive.

The prince leaned forward both to answer Fairy the First's question and feign courage. But his body betrayed him with trembling as he spoke, "Was the second creature really Gibby? I mean the true Princess Bridget? Surely it was changeling or shadow ... "

Fairy the First without pause, continued, "None of us have seen Bridget as she is the final night before a new moon, but we hear she is quite changed. What we need to know is ..."

Caedmon broke in on her line of questioning as a wave of angry nausea hit full force.

His voice rose, "You, ma'am, say, '*quite changed.*'" His tone now spit bitterness. "Cook said, 'she becomes something else altogether.' I ... cannot ... even ... speak of what I saw."

No amount of angry willpower could still his tremors now, but by the tone of his voice alone, Fairy the First fell silent. She did not drop her gaze.

Sometime in the midst of the standoff, Fairy the Fifth had stolen quietly forward and sat at Caedmon feet. She placed a strand of knotted yellow yarn across his open hand and drew it through again and again. Caedmon grasped it loosely and then took up the motion for himself. By this, and matching Fifth's breathing, he grew calm. Then, with empathy Caedmon would never forget, Fairy the Fifth took his face in her wrinkled fingers and said, "Bridget comes to us from time to time when the moon is waning—the time she prepares to enter her great suffering—but none of us have seen what you have." Caedmon broke from the steely gaze of Fairy the First and looked deeply into the eyes of the Fifth. She continued, "You bear the full brunt of Bridget's horror alone. Your need for camaraderie is well-founded. Our abilities are paltry in face of such need. We are sorry."

Stillness fell for some time. Then the sweet company cracked under the weight of Caedmon's sorrow. The fairies gave up the beautiful silence and turned to explaining.

"She is not getting any better but worse," sighed Fairy the Second to the others.

"It is our fault for not acting with more courage," said Fairy the Third.

"It was the palace staff and her parents," said Fairy the Fourth, "they spoiled her to the point of ruining her soul."

And round they went making points, strengthening positions, countering and agreeing, while Caedmon sat helpless, a man-in-love mourning. For a full quarter hour the discussion carried on until First's voice came crashing. "Blame, blame, blame," she bellowed, "The princess has a free will and she chose. She continues to choose. Let us not torture the young man any further."

Fairy the First then turned to Caedmon. "Young man, you have no obligation in this story. It is great and terrible and tangled. It would be easier to pull apart the labyrinth of the roof above us—and our ceiling is wrought from deep magic—than to play a part in the redemption of the lost princess of Endelion. You are welcome to stay here. But I doubt our fractious mothering will aid your recovery." Here First paused to glower at the others. "Our hospitality is at your disposal and that is more than we offered any of the other would-be suitors. Feel no shame for your inability. Everyone is limited. As for my advice —hold your first night with the princess close to your heart. It was a thing of beauty and beauty is never to be regretted."

Most of her words bounced off Caedmon but he nodded, the traditional man-price for buying silence. He then nodded again, head bobbling, in overwhelmed sleepiness. All five glanced his way and saw steady breathing, lips parted.

A second rocker was scooted round to face his seat and his feet were lifted upon it. Caedmon did not feel his boots pulled off. He did not hear the suggestion he be moved to Nanny's room. He did not notice the shushing and whispers of "Let sleeping princes lie."

A CHOICE OF THREE

THE DOG SNORED near the hearth. The night had grown cool. A pair of hands slipped the knotted yarn through Caedmon's boot strap, tied it snugly in a woodsman's loop, and then covered him with a blanket. The coverlet was handmade over the long life of a dozen fairies, a weave known only to their folk. Its patchwork pattern, threaded through silver and gold, would have kept a less tired man awake tracing the weave shown even in the dark.

Caedmon had not slept in a rocker since his mother held him as an infant. He had not slept so well since her death and slipped into his first vivid dream in years.

He floated in a vast night sky, moon and stars twirling about him. He spied, just below on a snowy hill, a wrinkled sage full of years standing between sputtering campfire and a telescope. Astronomical charts, multiple protractors, plumb lines, and compasses of varying size were piled on the bare ground at his feet. The wise man muttered philosophical mysteries and unfolding secrets of the ever-expanding universe. He predicted the movements of solar systems with intense precision as he charted the dance of the Milky Way. All at once in a high tenor voice he began to sing a cryptic verse of past and present. Amidst this depth of knowledge came an invitation to join, "Come prince, learn, understand, and rejoice!" Caedmon wondered what enigmas might be unraveled and mysteries unlocked if he were to sit at the feet of such a teacher.

But a long night of much-needed rest was not to be.

"Change of plans," called out Fairy the First, shaking Caedmon, handing him his boots and staff before his eyes came fully opened. "So sorry. No rest for the weary after all. But at least we got your belly filled." Bleary-eyed, Caedmon pulled on his boots and stood, not sure where he was or where to station himself. His footwear nagged at him for it shod opposite feet, but he was in no state of mind to pinpoint the discomfort.

All five hostesses were reentering the great room, wide-eyed and erect.

"Gwyllion!" they whispered one after the other. "She comes."

"There is no time to get you out the way you came," instructed Fairy the Second. "She's been tracking you for days. We'll have to use the pictures."

She led Caedmon to three egg-tempera paintings hanging opposite the hearth. Each was the length and breadth of a man's forearm, elbow to fingertip. Caedmon had not noticed them the evening before and wondered, scratching his head stupidly, at the apparent midnight rush to decorate. Second's tone was terse and firm. "Choose and go quickly!" she hissed, and then returned to her station to stand battle-ready.

Fairy the Third joined Caedmon at his left sleeve and took him closer in towards the gallery. She whispered, "Choose the left picture. It will put you back in your rightful place. A place from which you can set all things right." She pointed to the west-most painting and returned to her station, somber at full attention.

The west-most picture, delicate and nuanced, was of his grandfather's throne room in Morganstow. A crowd was bowing towards an empty throne. A palette of forlorn colors showed the deep-felt loss of a nation's sovereign. An emotional wave arose in Caedmon, mingling responsibility, nostalgia, sorrow, and repressed reprisal. He trembled as it crashed over him.

Fairy the Fourth joined Caedmon before the paintings and tugged on his right sleeve. She whispered, "Choose the right picture. It holds the key to your lady's heart. All you need to know to break the curse lies here." She pointed to the east-most painting, then returned to her station and stood vigilant.

The east-most composition was of his starlit dream in all its glorious detail, sage and telescope, moon and stars. Framed in white, the well-lit night sky danced around a familiar moon. It is as my dream foretold! Caedmon thought. A feeling of mystical premonition washed over him.

Fairy the Fifth joined him from behind, put a hand on each shoulder and turned Caedmon's body to face the center picture. He recognized it at once. Hilda's house and Hilda's lawn glimmered just before the dawn. It emanated its own light, jetting out into the surrounding dark, beast-filled forest, seeming even to cast a glow into the tension-filled, fairy-filled room where he stood.

He looked about for more guidance, torn. But none of his five hostesses took note of him any longer. They all faced outward, wide-stanced, soldiers ready for battle. Each held a staff, each of a different wood—an alder, a hickory, a chestnut, an oak, and a yew.

Prince Caedmon was left alone with the burden of choice. He bent to switch his boots as he prepared to make the leap. As he crouched, he fingered the knotted yarn to calm his head and heart. Then he rose and stepped through. By his departure he spared the five fairies much.

When Gwyllion burst in to Fairy Bower, not a prince was to be found, dog nor man. For when Caedmon stepped through frame and wall, on his heels came his hound.

[17]

WEAPONS AND WOUNDINGS

CAEDMON'S PRAYERS were answered with a resounding "no." He had prayed to land in the straight-backed chair beside the fire in Hilda's house, or better yet, to touch down with a splash into the comfort of a warm tub in the room beside her kitchen. But when the prince came through the painting, he was many miles from either comfort.

Still, the familiar woods were a solace, the staff of Hilda in his hand an even greater one. But what most lightened his heart was the company of four-legged Prince. Through no effort of his own, he had been chosen. Caedmon did not understand but was grateful for the mercy. "The first priority before we start, my traveling companion, is to rename you. Pardon the demotion, but I dub thee Duke. One prince is enough and, trust me, being a prince in this country is a headache."

The prince rubbed the duke's ears. The duke wagged his tail. Demotion accepted.

The companions stepped out on the journey, Duke following instead of leading this time. He knew at once these were Caedmon's woods and not his.

184

Night was falling fast. The moon was waning from her fullness and Caedmon trembled a little. Even though no longer in the kingdom of Endelion, he could not help but wonder how Bridget fared that night and whether she remained in gold or chose another color, reserving the regal hue for the height of her glory. He fought to remember her beauty and to resist the corroding shock of her deterioration. The memory of interacting inside her cottage hungered to swallow up all recollection of their first acquaintance. The moments of her dance under the stars seemed a fragile childish fantasy held up against the ugliness of her rage-filled other self. Pain stood stark and real.

The nourishment of fairy food and the straightforward honesty of their company had restored his mind and body. The moon lit the way and the staff, a familiar guide and balm, seemed eager to return home. Caedmon ran his thumb mindlessly over the almond-shaped knot, a habit fast becoming engrained. The wood gave a little. His hand paused, anxious that the precious gift had been wounded through his nervous tic, somehow marred by familiarity. Caedmon heard a muted pop and felt the release of a catch. He gasped as the precious staff came apart in his hands.

Instead of ragged scrap and jagged kindling, out from between the pieces of the staff came, with the lightest pull, a blade hidden within. The parting of the two ends unsheathed masterfully crafted steel. A sword gleamed in the starlight. Training from his youth flooded back. Though he was no champion, he was competent. All princes of Morganstow were mandated lessons in swordplay and Caedmon knew a good blade when he held one. With the discovery of the magnificent weapon, a facet of his childhood was handed back—redeemed, cold, hard, real.

The dog cowered.

"Bad history with swordplay, Duke?"

Duke whimpered.

"Back in the sheath it goes, boy."

Duke relaxed.

"I wonder what else Mother Hilda held back," Caedmon said aloud to his dog. "I did not listen to her as well as I should," he confessed. "I shall do differently this time round."

That night, as man and beast lay against one another, bedding down to sleep, Caedmon pondered, This time ... next time ... so often there is no next time. But I am heading through the woods to Hilda's house for a third time. He dozed off, thankful for both the destination and for knowing, for once, his aim.

Rising hours before dawn, duke and prince made good progress. This time there was no hiding in hollow trees, tripping over fallen branches, or doubling back. Three hours before the light of dawn, they were three miles from their destination.

But then came the wolves.

CAEDMON KNEW wolves were in the woods, but had given them no thought. The ferocious punishers did not pertain to him. He was traveling towards and not away from the pack's great nemesis, the unassailable lady of the cottage. But still, against all belief, a pack of wolves came. He was not an urchin rebel barreling headlong, full of his own import, screeching about an ogress. Yet the howls and hunger approached ever closer. Caedmon's last clear thought before the battle began was, But wolves sink their teeth into those running *away* from Mother Hilda ... His philosophy crumbled in the face of fear and fang.

Three factors saved Caedmon from the pack that closed in,

Duke being first. Dog knows dog. As the two travelers passed between the gaps in a cluster of elms, Duke emitted a low growl and all fur stood on end. The warning was all Caedmon needed to find the almond latch and unsheathe his blade. This time, at the sight of the great sword, Duke did not cower.

The weapon, and knowledge of its use, was Caedmon's second saving grace. Without blade and skill they would have been devoured.

The pack was a dozen thick and had not eaten for days. A man and his dog would be enough meal for several. Duke went into the midst of them, and by doing so both thinned the pack and, for a time, rendered Caedmon's sword useless. He dared not thrust the blade into the fray for fear of piercing his friend. His dread was well-founded. Upon seeing a she-wolf in full frenzy with Duke by the throat, Caedmon slashed through the remaining mayhem and pierced her through in a single thrust. But in the midst of that inescapable carnage, he cut a deep gash into his own dog. Duke's yelp and his master's cry of remorse rang though the forest. Caedmon flung his blade from him, fell to his knees, and felt to find and stop the flow of blood.

The Prince of Morganstow's reverberating grief unnerved the remaining four attackers. Leaderless, they hesitated. And in this space a third and final grace arrived. Three arrows in quick succession flew, arcing overhead, each hitting a mark. The fourth and final wolf scampered away as the young archer drew nearer, knife drawn and ready. Caedmon had removed the knotted rope from his boot strap and had applied it to Duke's leg as a tourniquet. He had hardly noticed the fall of the last three wolves, had not taken in the source of the flying arrows, when a new comrade heaved Duke to his shoulders and grunted one word, "Follow."

It took some minutes to find his sword again but soon it was sheathed. Then Caedmon turned and took out after the man who shouldered his dog. Half a mile out he caught up and found the stranger standing unsure. The path had forked.

"It is your turn to follow," Caedmon said, pushing past, his voice toneless with exhaustion. "I have her staff." The young man's blue eyes brightened when he saw the glowing staff of Hilda. A hint of envy entered his slight smile as he nodded and took up the rear.

The remainder of the way Caedmon led, but his new comrade refused to share the burden of carrying Duke. Caedmon was too tired to argue.

The moon was setting and the sun rising when Hilda's cottage came into view. Caedmon's heart rose aloft as if the cottage was his childhood abode. He wiped a silent tear that rolled down his cheek, thankful it was the eye opposite and out of view of his brave companion.

As THE THREE stepped into the final quarter mile, now and again they heard a rustle in the brush behind. Whatever followed was no wolf pack and smaller threats could wait. At the base of the hill below the cottage, Caedmon attempted a princely order, "Mother Hilda only accepts one guest at a time. Go."

His order was refused with a firm shake of the head. "I will tend to the dog in the shepherd's hut by the barn."

Caedmon recognized intractable stubbornness so he acquiesced adding, "His name is Duke."

"Yes, sir."

"And your name?"

"Albius."

"I am Caedmon."

"I know."

The two parted and the prince continued alone up the hill towards home.

As he mounted the hill, a wall of silence greeted him. No cricket chirped. No mourning dove cooed. The holy hush was beckoning him into its sacred activity but Caedmon's heart was far from quiet. His only thought was the pounding question of the wolves. Why the attack? Why the violence? Why bloodshed and injury of the innocent? He felt certain Mother Hilda would know. She, after all, had power over wolves.

With great strides he hastened his pace, advancing across the lawn. He took the staff and rapped loudly on the front door. The latch gave way and Caedmon barreled into the candlelit room where Hilda sat, face towards the hearth. The griefs of his journey cried out, presuming audience was due him. The long-lost beloved Caedmon had returned. But Hilda did not move.

Peering round fireside to see what absorbed her so, Caedmon started. Mother Hilda's face was ageless and godlike and rather than the bright eyes of green he had come to know, flashing orbs of radiance reflected in rapid succession all the great many worlds on display in the gallery of the great hall.

OF DOGS AND WOLVES

MIDDAY, Hilda brought lunch to the young men out in the shepherd's hut. Caedmon glanced up and then away mumbling his thanks. As she left, she reached for the staff, commenting, "There's wolves' blood to be cleaned from the blade." Caedmon no longer felt worthy to hold it so it was just as well. He focused instead on his wounded dog.

Both Duke and Hilda loved Caedmon, but before them both he now felt ashamed and small. He did not deserve the loyalty of the dog he had wounded. He did not deserve the help of the woman whose privacy he had invaded. Twice over he was a desecrator of holy ground.

Duke was unable to walk but there was much hope of recovery. For this, Caedmon thanked his new friend. Albius was an ever-changing mix of warm and wary. His black hair and blue eyes contrasted sharply with Caedmon's auburn locks and deep brown irises.

"Your place is in the house," Caedmon argued. But Albius shrugged. "I've had a fortnight of personalized attention before your arrival. The bed is wondrous, the bath is miraculous, but she sees the inner soul. After awhile, it feels intrusive. The constant whittling away ... I fear there will be nothing I know of myself left."

Caedmon sensed in his fellow guest an exhaustion that echoed his own. Both were at Hilda's house sharing the burden of nursing a faithful friend back to life. It was bond enough. Neither were in the mood for backstories and here in the shepherd's hut, social rank meant nothing.

The morning of their second day of being thrown together, Caedmon inquired, "How long do you plan to stay, Albius?"

"I came for a mending but have found no miracle cure. I think to go when your dog is out of danger. Perhaps tomorrow or the day after." His reply invited no further inquiry. "What about you?"

"I sense I have little say in the matter." answered Caedmon.

"We can choose to leave whenever we like," countered Albius with more energy than usual, and more bite than he intended.

"Yes, that is true. We are free, but I have found I have little sense of when it is best to leave," Caedmon returned.

"Say more," invited Albius, hoping to fall back into listening.

"Oh, what do I know?" sighed Caedmon, rubbing his eyes with his palms.

From here followed fresh arguments as to who would sleep where: who in the hut and who in the house. Then the weather removed the dilemma. A thunder clap and a downpour enclosed their dwelling and both became thankful for the sturdiness of wall and roof.

At the second thunder clap a scratching was heard at the door. To their amazement, Duke lifted his head. His tail thumped weakly signaling a welcome. Both men noted the improvement and in a single parting motion Caedmon went to his dog as Albius to the door.

A wounded wolf lay soaked and half-dead on the stoop. Albius hesitated and looked back at Duke. The shepherd dog did not raise his head again but gave a single satisfactory thump of his tail. The wolf was brought in and the ratio of human to canine, patient to attendant, became one to one.

Duke's patches of fawn and black contrasted sharply with the young wolf's black on black, but the two hounds did not differ greatly in size. Caedmon's eyes grew wide as the wolf was set down by the dog. He shuddered in the presence of yet another unknown.

"It's not so unlike a dog as you might think," said Albius, self-assured.

"You've done this before?" returned his companion with one brow raised.

Alibis nodded but once.

The two canines' wounds were not unalike. Bite marks around the neck, a single gash from Caedmon's sword in the foreleg. The blood-soaked bandages doubled but the comfort of a fellow sufferer accelerated the healing somehow.

For three days the rain continued. Bread and fresh bandages appeared in the window but neither man saw Mother Hilda come or go. Albius jokingly called the young wolf Earl and the name stuck. His black eyes grew bright like his master's blue.

"I'm surrounded by royalty," laughed the dark-headed young man. "Prince, Duke, and now Earl."

"And you listed your comrades in opposite order of rank," Caedmon quipped. "More troubling, you prefer the earl over the duke, and the prince is little more than your head nurse. You, my good sir, are on political thin ice."

Albius froze and looked down. "I do not mean to offend."

Caedmon realized his joke had struck a nerve. "Look at me," he ordered.

Albius obeyed, blue eyes meeting brown.

"You saved my life. You are saving my dog's life. There is no rank in this room."

Both men breathed deeply. Then tensions from old memories exited with two long exhales, like smoke rings from weighty peace pipes.

For three days and four nights they broke bread together and watched beloved dogs regain strength. In the evenings a small fireplace provided some warmth. On the fourth and final night, Albius whistled a tune and then, overcome by the beauty of the melody, sang out as he sat by the flickering fire—

> *A man's a friend who greets a man*
> *And tells the bitter truth*
> *A woman's a riddle*
> *She be no friend*
> *My poor heart aches as proof*
>
> *A lovely wife might cure me*
> *But I might treat her cruel*
> *She instead could drive me mad*
> *And I might play the fool*
>
> *I'm a deaf and dumb and desperate man*
> *Too much myself both ill and good*
> *Love bar the door from bitterness*
> *I don't do as I should*
> *I ought, I might, I could*

CAEDMON LEARNED QUICKLY and joined him in the second chorus—

> *A lovely wife might cure me*
> *But I might treat her cruel*
> *She instead could drive me mad*
> *And I could play the fool*

A passerby might have looked in and thought the two men drunk. But Mother Hilda had supplied no wine past the bitter stuff for tending wounds.

The fourth morning the sun shone, the dogs ate upon all fours, and each man took a turn going out and stretching two legs.

[19]

OF WOLVES AND MEN

WHEN THE RAIN RELENTED, the two young men and Mother Hilda met together and an ordered arrangement for living was agreed upon. A night in the simple luxury of the cottage, each man taking his turn in the bath and warm bed, then a night in the hut training the hounds. Finally, every third night, into the forest two men and two dogs would go. Mother Hilda, though not unwelcoming of Earl, wanted to see if he would remain with Albius or return to his old home and own kind.

Duke provided Earl a margin more incentive to stay, a new pack of sorts. Each man had grown to love Earl and were surprised by his eager responsiveness and obedience. The nights in the woods were an unexpected pleasure: fireflies, stars, and the occasional hunt. They shared silent company, the pleasure of dogs, and the hope that Earl would continue to choose his new masters over the wildness of his past. Caedmon held close a small un-thought-through fear that the bond between the dogs was so intense that Duke might follow Earl into the wilds of the forest and never return.

Three weeks in, Mother Hilda broke the pattern. She met

the men as they climbed out of the forest and up the hill, addressing them one at a time.

"Albius, we are in good standing?"

"Yes, Mother," he replied with no hesitation.

"Get some rest. Tonight Kassia will try to come to us and she will need your help, much the same manner as Caedmon did. You must return to the forest as two, not four. Earl will go with you and be put to the test."

Alibis nodded, pondering.

Small world, thought Caedmon, but said nothing. Mother Hilda now looked towards him.

"Caedmon, it is time to ready you for what is next."

"Shall I come straight on to the house?"

Hilda nodded. She turned and spoke then to Duke, giving the dog more leeway than either human. "Duke, you may go or stay as you please." Duke hardly knew what to do with the freedom. He whined at Mother like one begging for orders.

Albius moved towards the shepherd's hut, Earl at his heel. Caedmon went towards the stately cottage, smiling satisfied. Two he loved, it seemed, might love each other. Kassia was joining them and it would be good to see her again.

An agitated Duke raced back and forth between the men, yipping and whining. Choice tortured the animal. In the end, his body remained at Hilda's cottage with Caedmon while his mind and heart raced in the wood with Albius and Earl.

When Caedmon reached the cottage, there was no need to knock. Mother Hilda stood by the open door. Without words she directed him to clean himself then eat. Together they supped in silence. Only when the dishes were scraped clean did she motion for him to join her in front of the fire. Last he'd seen her there her eyes were altogether other. A creeping sense of dread came upon him.

"You shake," Mother began. Caedmon clasped both hands

trying to stop. "And the trembling shall continue as long as the moon, *her* moon has hold," she added.

Caedmon wondered, but was not surprised by all Hilda already knew. Her words described his despair, but in her tone was the gentle cradling of hope. "Is there no cure? Time perhaps?" asked Caedmon, daring not to look into her great green eyes.

"Time is often our friend but it never stands on its own. You left Endelion, but a piece of you stayed behind."

"If only I had not leapt into the portrait, consumed by beauty. If only I had stayed and learned from you longer before leaving, I might have had the strength to save her." Two tears ran down silent cheeks. Oh, Mother Hilda, I am so weary of my crying, he wanted to add, but did not.

"Yes, you left *me* too soon," she replied. "You left your princess of Endelion just in time. You cannot save the creature that broke your heart. B would have consumed you if you had remained. She consumes all who enter her hut."

"Mother!" Caedmon sat straight up. Hope arose on a boyish face. "*You. You* could go! *You* could teach her ... reach her."

Hilda remained silent and left the silence alone.

The clock struck. Duke barked. Mother checked on him through the open window and then returned to sit by the prince.

"Do you not remember the first night we met? Loman running wild in the forest?"

"Twice, Mother. Twice I watched."

"Do you still think I can bend human will? He was a child, and with young ones there is hope even for hard cases. Bridget is now a woman."

"Perhaps if I brought her here ...?" Caedmon pressed,

though less emphatically, "At your house she could be cured. I was. And my wounds were deep."

Hilda reached and took his hand, kissed it gently, and held it in her lap.

"Your wounds were deep ... are still deep, but not like hers, dear Caedmon. She would have to *choose* to come to me, and choose while at her worst, in the height of her ugliness, minutes before the turning away of the new moon."

Both Caedmon and Hilda stared into the fire watching it crackle. The great teapot sat and spat but refused to whistle.

Hilda spoke again, "She is threaded through your heart, but tell me how your heart is when it stands in solitude before my fire."

Caedmon sat for a moment more, then stood, staring at the flames. He walked to the corner where Hilda had laid the newly polished staff, lifted it, twirled it once and carried it back towards the hearth. By the fire once more, he laid it to rest high across the great stone mantle. The wood and stone ennobled each other, one on display, the other displaying.

"I am a man without a home, Mother. I belong neither to Endelion nor Morganstow. If I cannot win her, or at least free her, then my home is here in service to you. I will guard your forest and bring those I can to your house of healing."

Mother's eyes were bright with love. "I am blessed that you would express such a desire. To be a woodsman of Hilda House requires long grinding obedience and will try you in ways the quest for a princess does not. But whichever path lies in your future, you cannot continue to suffer the wound received from Bridget's other self."

"What wound?" asked Caedmon, scanning himself. "I closed the door before she could grab hold."

"And it is a mercy you escaped a second touch, or you could

do little more now than shake—never mind fighting wolves and healing them."

Caedmon pondered her answer. He did not argue.

"What is the cure?" he asked at last.

"Listen closely, prince of Morganstow, when I answer. I do not, and never will, speak to you of Bridget's cure. Though you want her wholeness with all your heart, you must seek only your own. When you go to her, and that is where I am sending you, it is to say goodbye."

A look of wisdom fell over Caedmon, newly heard but long-time known.

"When I say goodbye, can the moon be full?"

"We cannot hold and choose our times, Caedmon. Cycles and seasons are different in each world and rarely are they in sync."

Mother paused, and then continued, "All I know is the time is now, but I pray for your sake the moon is anything but new. That is the one space of time in which Bridget cannot hear 'goodbye' any more than she can hear 'hello' or 'I love you.' She is then in her inmost person, where the wound owns the soul, where each stands naked and alone. I think you have experienced enough not to lie to yourself in this matter and play the hero. If the moon is new, you must run."

Caedmon nodded. And shivered.

Hilda put her hand on his shoulder. "You saw what no one else has. It is a lonely burden, hard to be borne."

"I understand, Mother, what *not* to do. What is it that I should do instead?"

"You are going to remake a memory, to recapture the good of your first meeting. Find her as she is. Love her as she is. Strengthen her as she is. Bless her, and say goodbye."

A BARK CALLED OUT. A bark came in return.

Hilda and Caedmon stood together and walked to a west facing window. Albius was coming up the hill carrying his Kassia, her arms wound tightly around his happy neck. He was radiant and singing. Earl came after, and Duke ran to greet them both. The great wolf was limping but his tail wagged in triumph.

Mother Hilda whispered, "Earl has fought his own pack for the sake of his new master. A double redemption has been wrought this night."

"Is Kassia okay?" asked Caedmon.

"*That* is not your business," Hilda admonished. "We must send you on your way *now*."

Caedmon lifted the staff from the mantle and entered the great hall. Albius's song poured through and filled the cottage. As Caedmon stepped through the frame, the tune attempted to follow—

> *Mother! my darling is quite alive*
> *Two years of waiting felt like ten*
> *A million deaths my hope survived*
> *To come alive again!*

[20]

NEVER TO RETURN

ONCE THROUGH THE PAINTING, Caedmon looked for the moon. But the night sky was overlaid with a thick low ceiling of clouds. A murky mist haunted the forest and fields as if sorrowing after something unnameable. Caedmon's hopes had been set on a full moon, a quick goodbye, followed by a short reunion with the fairies. He remembered the fear on their faces and their cry of "She comes!" He wished to kiss each cheek and assure himself of no further losses. But navigation was near impossible. The foggy conditions held for a day and a night and another day with no sign of change.

The prince of Morganstow may have navigated through the mists in his homeland but, besides the trail between Bridget's cottage and the royal palace, the forests of Endelion were strange to him. The fog added to his tired confusion and this time there was no help from Duke.

His first brush with familiarity was a near fall. The roots of the yew he had inhabited in his bitter night of hopelessness entangled his feet. Its branches evoked the memory of his last travels towards Gibby. He had intended then only to say goodbye. The landmark brought little comfort. He dared not enter the yew's shelter again lest the spirit of despair revisit him. He slept in the open but fitfully.

Caedmon knew more, much more, than last he came to Endelion, but the knowledge made him sober rather than confident. Wise experience was useless in the fog. Though Hilda's staff gave light, he could not discern its leading as he would have liked. With no better plan, he trudged on into day two.

CAEDMON HAD JUST BEGUN to content himself with walking in circles when he found he knew exactly where he stood. He had been ushered into the center of a circular grove, a perfectly circular grove. Five razed trunks were barely discernible in the soft green glow of staff-light. An alder, a chestnut, a hickory, an oak, and a yew had once stood tall. The roots remained deep, the circumferences symmetrical, the spacing perfect. And now each stood at identical heights—that of a man's shins. Branches intertwined no more, for none remained.

Where once floated the majestic domed roof was now an empty haze. On clear nights, Caedmon supposed, a thousand twinkling stars would be in view. Turf and moss lay like ash. Stones were strewn about where walls once stood. The smokeless chimney still stood, propped between uncut birch and beech. There the prince saw dangling a slat from a picture frame, no longer than a man's forearm from elbow to fingertip. It balanced precariously on a corner of the mantle, a smudge of egg tempera smeared along its bottom edge.

The ash stump-turned-dining-table was now a fire pit. Not a root remained. From the gaping hole smoke still puffed, lingering miniatures of what used to float from the hearth out the magnificent chimney.

Caedmon sat upon the oak, unable to imagine the violence needful for such destruction. Former glory was now charcoal and kindling. He glanced about for bones and bodies commensurate with the battle that must have raged, but was met with nothing but stillness and sorrow. Grief hung in the air, weaving through the black haze and ever-present fog.

Should the living stumps give hope? he wondered. Should the annihilated ash give satisfaction?

What little in the way of plans he had carried into Endelion, what little hope he had of returning, now wafted skyward between stumps of once beloved trees. The fumes and smoke stung his eyes, which were now exhausted of all tears.

Dawn would be here soon, but as yet there was no streak of light. Caedmon stood to leave, leaning hard upon the staff. It flickered in the tightness of his grip. He turned in several directions trying to choose a course for his tired feet, dreading the merciless wood and the treading of its lonely pathways in his solitary plight. No hound had leapt through after him this time.

Caedmon at last chose a direction and moved towards the space between alder and yew. There the yellow door had once swung inward. He would exit in the same way he came in those many weeks before. As he stepped across the threshold, he heard a moan. The prince spun on his heel to catch the sound a second time, but his heart betrayed all hearing by pounding in his ears. A suggestion of life seemed to be coming from the hearth and a second and third groan led him straight to the fireplace. There lay, in a crumpled darkened heap, a human form. By the fluttering light of the staff he perceived the countenance of an old woman. A blackened cloak and hood concealed her hair, and her eyes were tight shut. Which of the fairies? Under what bewitchment? How wounded was she in the great war of five against one?

The prince took off his coat and wrapped it round her.

Consumed by compassion and thankful for company of any sort, Caedmon cared not if he were nurturing Gwyllion herself. He thought of the tender benevolence of Mother Hilda and felt her watchful guiding eye. No more did he spin directionless. He would take her to Nanny and Cook. They would know what to do.

The staff was cinched against princely back, freeing both arms to cradle an aged woman. He had not gone twelve paces out of the ring of ruin, a stone's throw from the stumps, when eyelids fluttered. Tears rose and flowed down her grey wrinkled cheeks, but she spoke not a word. Eyes closed tight again, yet tears flowed on. Her whole appearance was so utterly pitiful that Caedmon was near crying too.

"Oh, sweet little mother, what is the matter?" he said in a pleading whisper. "I promise to do all I can to help." She seemed to have fallen asleep but he continued his comforting whispers. Belted tight, the staff shone down over his head onto the path, brighter than ever before. As if aware of the pressing need, the green light darkened with every misstep and brightened with every step well-chosen.

Caedmon's burden weighed very little. He flew as if her life depended upon his speed. They were not far from the edge of the wood when her tears began to flow yet faster and she gave such a sad moan that it went to Caedmon's very heart.

"Mother, mother!" he said. "Poor little mother!" And he then bent and kissed her on her withered lips. She started but Caedmon took no notice, pressing on to make his way through the last tangled grove of trees between him and the palace.

As he broke into the clearing, the palace in full view, his burden began to move. She grew so cumbersome in her restlessness that it became impossible to carry her a moment longer. Caedmon bent to lay her on the grass where they both might rest a moment.

But as the sun rose, so did his charge.

The light glided down the hill, cutting a swath in the clouds fleeing before its luminous presence, and the woman stood upright on her feet. As Caedmon turned his face from the direction of the palace, he saw her hood drop back from her face and flowing hair. He watched as her tresses fell about her and the first dawn of morning caught her face. The loveliest eyes matched to perfection the sky's darkest blue. He recoiled in overmastering wonder.

It was Bridget.

She was the woman in the chimney, his burden of compassion. He fell at her feet weeping in disbelief. He had indeed kissed her without knowing it.

Four days before, the moon had been waning, creeping ever closer to her time of hiddenness. The princess had wandered sickly and afraid towards the flight of fairies that had been at her christening. They had so often cared for her and she sought them once again. Arriving, Bridget had found only their chimney and had no strength for return to her cottage. There she had lain herself, crumpled in the hearth, waiting to make her acquaintance with death.

Now Princess Bridget of Endelion raised Prince Caedmon of Morganstow to his feet. She laid her right hand upon his left cheek. She laid her left hand upon his right cheek. Staring into his deep brown tear-filled eyes she murmured, "You kissed me when I was an old woman. I kiss you now when I am a young princess."

Too soon she broke away. Even Caedmon's lips could not forever compete with a glorious sunrise. Looking into the glowing east, Bridget cried, "Is that the sun coming?!"

"Indeed it is, my dearest," returned Prince Caedmon. And wishing his wondering bride to be in his arms, he scooped her aloft and carried her towards the palace singing—

> *Nightfall's gone, O come and see*
> *I've kissed my lovely bride*
> *From curse and sorrow been set free*
> *No more her face to hide*
>
> *Oh petals shut, begin to bloom*
> *Delight my darling's eyes*
> *In midnight sorrow once entombed*
> *She greets the clear blue skies*
>
> *With sunlight fill our souls with hope*
> *Buds laughing now increase*
> *Cascading down the gentle slope*
> *Entwine past pains in peace.*

COOK AND NANNY stood in the doorway watching them come.
Each had an arm around the other, cheeks streaked and salty.